Maine
Under Water

Maine
Under Water

Allison Whittenberg

Apprentice
House Press
Loyola University Maryland

First Edition

Hardcover ISBN: 978-1-62720-516-0
Paperback ISBN: 978-1-62720-517-7
Ebook ISBN: 978-1-62720-518-4

Design by Eisa Abu-Sbaih
Editorial Development by Enrique Muchacho
Promotion Development by Maddie Holmes

Published by Apprentice House Press

Loyola University Maryland
4501 N. Charles Street, Baltimore, MD 21210
410.617.5265
www.ApprenticeHouse.com
info@ApprenticeHouse.com

Also by Allison Whittenberg

Sweet Thang
Hollywood and Maine
Life is Fine
Tutored
Sane Asylum
Carnival of Reality

To Marlowe

Chapter 1

Life is a series of moments; the problem with that fact is that most of these moments happen like blips on a screen, so you pay little attention to them. Rarely does something <u>great</u> happen. June 12, 1976, that was my time (almost). I had been working for that moment since 7th grade. Thanks to all my study, all my struggle and toil, it was tabulated that I had the highest GPA of my graduating class. Out of fifty-eight students, I was on top. Not monumental odds, I know, but it meant something to me.

It seemed half of my hometown was crammed into our combination cafeteria/gymnasium/auditorium that evening. Squeaky, gray steel seats were set up in closed rows. Big fans were stationed at each corner and churned out an air flow to counter the stuffy humidity that hung in the cramped room.

From the makeshift stage, I surveyed the crowd and caught my dad's eye. He winked at me. Beside him was my ma and younger (by a year) brother Leo. Next to him, my cousin, obnoxious seven-year-old Tracy John, was fidgety, annoyed in the outfit my ma had made him wear. His complaint: come Sunday he was going to have to wear a stiff, pressed shirt and tie again, and wasn't getting dressed up once a week enough?

My oldest brother Horace sat up straight. He was proud to show off his dress greens to the neighborhood. This was the first time he'd been back home from Hawaii all year.

On either side of me stood by two best friends, Cissy and Millicent. My boyfriend Raymond, who had the honor of being class salutatorian, had made opening remarks, but was now positioned over by the American flag. From time to time, I'd catch his gaze. He'd flash me that alligator smile I'd become so fond of, and I had to fight the urge to swoon. It would soon be my time in the bright light. I had to concentrate.

So, the march in was done and Principal Abderholden, a squat man in his fifties with a big round voice, had the mic in his hand in a vice-like grip. You'd think it was his day, not mine (I mean, ours). Didn't Principal Abderholden get enough airtime? He'd spoken on the intercom five days a week at both the opening and the closing of school plus every breaking announcement for the past dozen years.

On top of that, I didn't rate his words too highly. I realize not every speech could be as pithy as Lincoln's "Gettysburg Address", but I could have described his speech as boring as watching paint dry—that is, if I wanted to be that harsh to paint.

He spoke to us about hope. And, even though

everyone's for hope (I hope), Principal Abderholden lost me when he said he had "High hopes for the future" (as opposed to what—hope for the past?)

Then, Principal Abderholden talked about change. How entering senior high school was going to be "such a change, but we should not let this vast change, change us".

I looked down at my wristwatch.

It was going to change from 7:44 to 7:45 in about a minute. No, I was wrong. The big hand wasn't on the twelve.

It changed in twenty-five seconds.

Principal Aberholden also warned us, "After today, things will never be the same."

I had always been wary of people who say things like that. Not to get into quantum physics—but according to Sir Isaac Newton, things will always be in constant motion. That's nature's law.

"Parents, loved ones, teachers, and friends, we prepare to turn this page to a new chapter. We must forge ahead and seek to climb new mountains."

With that I thought he was winding down, but he then switched topics to the upcoming school merger.

"...And as fate would have it, this is also the end. The end of Dardon Junior High School."

Really? A school merger was an act of nature?

Of course, he could not deal with it to us straight. He couldn't give us the facts that our school was being torn down because it was 83 years old, rickety, and laden with lead paint. No, he had to garnish his sentences with mustard, ketchup, and relish. He had to go on and on and on about how people travel all around the world to see relics, but in America it's always out with the aged to make room for the new. (So, I guess he thought this building was our town's version of the Parthenon?) And wasn't that a pity because he himself had attended Dardon Junior High way back in 1949. Then, Mr. Abderholden got emotional. His voice broke in spots. "This ... school...."

Come on, man, pull it together.

A few people in the audience dabbed their eyes and covered their faces with their hands from the stark grief.

Were they actually crying real tears over an institution? A school is bricks and mortar, isn't it? Maybe, I had a heart of stone, but I didn't find it possible to get worked up about it. Those feelings for walls and ceilings and floors didn't surface with me.

"...I hope you will take a part of Dardon Junior High with you throughout your life wherever you go," Principal Abderholden told us. (Mental note: swing by during the demolition and pocket a few pieces of rubble as a keepsake.) "Because even though this is not the best school and there are many, many, many things that we lack; it is and will always be our school. Please welcome the valedictorian 1976 for the last graduating class of Dardon Junior High —"

What a segue, Mr. Abderholden.

"Charmaine Upshaw."

There was applause and a few shouts of my name, but I didn't advance. I wasn't sure the principal was finished.

He finally stepped away from the microphone, and I crept to the foreground.

We shook hands as we crossed each other. As I approached the lectern, my cap slipped off. I'd had it secured with a thousand bobby pins, but it came loose all the same. I don't think the designers of this type of haberdashery were anticipating the afro. After picking the cap up from the floor and enduring a few random snickers, I regrouped and let it all sink in. So what if that square hat didn't jibe with my kinky hair, this was what I'd been waiting the entire fourteen years of my life for. I threw my shoulders back and tilted my chin forward.

Before I started my speech, I thanked my ma and daddy for being my ma and daddy. Then, I acknowledged my older brother Horace, not for existing as my big brother, but for his whopping seven months of service to this nation.

Horace raised lifting one hand in the air in a grandiose 'all hail' gesture.

People clapped.

"Thank you, Horace," I said and motioned for him to park it.

Horace next stood and did a bow, and the crowd began to cheer even more for him.

"Seriously, Horace, sit down," I said.

Horace gave me a stiff-armed salute and returned to his seat.

As a civilian, I returned with a limp wave.

I thanked my other brother, my gammy, and two uncles that were in attendance then I eyed my cousin whose tan, cherubic face was upturned to me.

"To Tracy John with the big smile and personality," I said, "Thank you. I would also like to thank your mother, Karyn, the first Upshaw to ever go to college. I hope to follow in her footsteps."

When the applause died, I gripped the lectern and took a deep breath and unfolded the paper I held. I began, "Often in the annals of history...."

The lights went out.

I wish I were speaking metaphorically, but, unfortunately, I wasn't. Right then, there was a power outage.

The whole room went black, and I heard the scrambling of feet and the loud instruction of "Exit over here."

Behind me, my fellow classmates rushed away.

I stood there awash in denial. *This couldn't be happening*, I thought as I stared into the dark void that a few seconds ago was my captive audience.

Chapter 2

"Come on, Maine, this way," Tracy John said.

His little hand led me outside to what was left of the day's sunlight. There, I saw where the attendants of the proceedings escaped to. Usually, we got yelled at for standing on the grass, but that evening, due to the evacuation, we were allowed.

No one looked panicked. They milled about the school steps or the monument. Some had wandered as far as the corner.

'Must be a power outage' was the explanation I heard uttered repeatedly.

"The circuits get overloaded during these hot mucky months," Daddy said. "People have more things turned on and the next thing you know the grids go kerplop."

"How long will the lights be out, Unc?" Tracy John asked.

"Hours, maybe."

I peered about and said, "If everyone would kind of get back into a circle, I could do my speech right here."

"There's no chance of that, Head of the Class," Horace told me, placing a hand on my shoulder. "This ceremony is over."

With that news, I unzipped my black gown. Under it, I wore a lavender dress and itchy, white tights over my too long, twig-like legs. Like my younger cousin, Ma had forced clothes on me. For this and all occasions, my vote had been for dungarees and a dashiki but, of course, I was vetoed.

"This is gonna be like last summer," Uncle O said. "There was a blackout every other week. The electric company does it on purpose."

I drifted away at that point because I knew things were going to veer into a full-fledged conversation on the energy crisis and Jimmy Carter and who in their right mind would want to hear about an electricity shortage on commencement night?

Happy to be in the cool evening air, clusters formed. Family members bunched around their graduates. The crowd now had a mind of its own. Horace was right; there was no regrouping. After a few more minutes, a couple of people even headed for their cars.

I made my way over to Millicent and her family. They mentioned how early she had to get up the next day. She had band camp.

My other best friend Cissy too was about to flee the confines of Dardon for the summer. She was going with her sister and niece to their new place in Delaware to help them get settled.

Two PTA members went back into the building with flashlights and rolled out with cake and punch.

Before I knew it, there was a food chain going. When a slice and a cup came my way, I passed on both. This was how fate worked; the lights didn't go out during Abderholden's drone or earlier that day during school when nothing consequential was going on besides last day board games. No, it had to happen in the first sentence of my prepared speech, one that I'd worked hours on. The one that I had this one chance, this one time.

It was graduation night; any other time would be irrelevant.

I moseyed back to where my folks were and Uncle O was at it still, this time he was yapping about OPEC and how they were hoarding all the oil, so the price would shoot up again.

"I don't know why we don't move to solar already," I said before making another round.

"At least, we'll get a few weeks out of it before they start taxing the sun."

Dinah, a self-professed beauty queen, flipped her Farrah Fawcett hair as she breezed past me. She was laughing, arm and arm with this guy Demetrius who I'd used to believe was a full-fledged dreamboat, now I concluded that he was dingy. Both pretended like they didn't know me. I frowned then shrugged. I guess there are some parts of junior high history I didn't mind ditching.

As people ate and drank, there was more talk about the impending merger.

"Well, at least the new school won't have these problems. It will be state of the art with the wall to wall carpeting and the central air," someone said.

"I bet that place will have a generator as backup," someone else said.

"That new school will have everything. That's how they do things for their kids."

I shook my head. I knew it wouldn't be long before that ~~was~~ gotten around to. The fact was not only that our redistricted school would be lead free, but it would also be racially integrated. Oliver L. Brown, parent of black third grader Linda Brown, went against the school board of Topeka, Kansas to try to get her a desk and chair at an all-white primary school. That was way back in 1954. You would think people would have gotten used to us by now but no. Racial desegregation was still a hot topic complete with all this hand wringing and nay saying some 22 years later. When would racial relations matter?

"You know they really don't want us there."

"You can say that again."

Thankfully, he didn't.

Another twenty minutes of shuffling went by but still no formal announcement of 'sorry folks but the shows over' was rendered.

At this rate, it didn't look good for my speech let alone none of us even got to walk the platform. Instead, when it got close to nine at night, Principal Abderholden handed out the diploma like a paper boy. (How unceremonious!) He weaved throughout the crowd calling out names "Tulane, Underwood, Upshaw…"

Still, I perked up as he winged mine to me. I guess it's better than having to wait to get it in the mail.

As I looked at the front of the document, I noticed a huge red blotch on it (great, during all this blackout chaos someone had spilled a punch on it).

Raymond came over to me right then. I had to hand it to him; he always looked on the bright side. "The important thing is that you earned the rank of valedictorian. They can't take that away from you."

I nodded.

I looked back down at the document. The ink had smudged where it stated my cumulative average.

Nevertheless, my boyfriend was right; it was nothing to fret over. It was a piece of paper. I was sure somewhere somehow I could get a new copy.

So, that was it for commencement. People hurried home to light their candles and salvage whatever hadn't gone bad in their fridge.

I took one last look at the faded red brick building with gray trim. I sighed.

So long, Dardon Junior High. Next time I see you, you will be reduced to rubble. What's the saying: it's been real, and it's been good. However, I wasn't sure if my junior high experience had been really good.

Chapter 3

No more pencils, no more books, no more teachers' dirty looks, was how the jingle went but already I found myself missing that grind and all that went with it. I was one of those freaks of nature that never liked the summer. It's too open. You have to make your own structure, create your own sense of fun, or else you're stuck watching reruns of <u>The Monkees</u>. I woke up the next morning early in order to make it to school only to find out there was no school, neither that day nor the day after. I was a free woman who longed to be tossed back into the institution.

There I was thinking, maybe, I shouldn't have tried so hard to be valedictorian. Maybe, I should have flunked a class or two because, at least, then I could have summer school to look forward to.

I crept downstairs to get my usual: shredded wheat. Ma was already busy in the kitchen making hominy grits. Her hair was tied back in a tight bun and the sleeves of her house dress rolled up to her elbows.

"Good Morning, New Graduate," Ma said in her deep Alabama accent. "You know, the lights didn't come back on till two last night."

Ma was bright, chirpy, and full of conversation, but I didn't pick up my end. I grunted instead of using words and went to the icebox in search of the carton. When I couldn't find it, I said, "Don't tell me, we're out of milk."

"I just got done telling you; the power's been off for hours. I had to throw the milk out."

"That's great," I said in a deflated voice as I sunk into a chair at the kitchen table.

"Haven't you heard, Charmaine?" she asked. "Not to cry over spoiled milk -"

I started to correct her that the saying was spilled not spoiled milk, but I nixed that and rolled my eyes as she prattled on -

"- I'm fixing to go to the store after the boys get up. You're welcome to come with me."

I began clinking the saltshaker together with the pepper shaker. "I don't want to go boring food shopping with you, Ma."

"Well, what do you want to do today?"

"I don't know."

"You don't know?" she asked and came out from behind the stove to me and stared me down. "You don't have any idea one way or another?"

"No, Ma, I don't," I said, rising from the table and heading back to the stairs to go back to my room.

"The hominy's almost ready. How about a nice bowl of that?"

"I don't want any hominy, Ma. I don't want anything to eat."

"Well, you gotta eat something."

"Do I?" I asked her from the staircase.

"Charmaine, please don't be a teenager," she called after me. "It'll be a long summer if you do."

Chapter 4

When you reach a certain age, you have to make your own excitement, that's the big drawback of being a teenager. You have all the responsibility without freedom.

Tracy John, who had just turned seven, was the exact opposite. Years away from involuntary servitude, he wasn't tied down at all.

That afternoon, Ma told me to take him to the YMCA because that day he was to see which swim class he qualified for. Tracy John could do butterfly, fly fish, front crawl, and backstroke, so I didn't worry much over his fate. As things went, he made it into the advanced "fish" class. Most of the kids who fit into that class were much bigger than him; some were even approaching my height. Quite an accomplishment for my cousin, still I thought of him that way as I did all swimmers: they were all a bunch of showoffs. So grand in their swim trunks and suits, believing that they had the upper hand (and kinda they did because the earth is two thirds water).

I was jealous of them because I never learned how. Over the years, I'd had my chances. But, unlike others who tried and mastered this skill, for me, it never came together – the arm movements, the leg kicks, and the breathing. I always found myself forgetting to do one thing or another and sinking. I was always second guessing myself, always so paralyzed with fear.

I wasn't a chicken, though. Well, about most things I wasn't.

Swimming didn't scare me because, theoretically, I understood the process. I could do the motions on dry land. It was all about the water. Though I'd never been in an ocean, a controlled environment to me was just as perilous. An Olympic sized pool held a lot of H2O. Surrounded by all that water, it would be a fight to stay afloat. Sure, the water went to nine feet, and there I was a freak of nature tall standing almost six feet (last time I measured). I knew I couldn't swim vertically, but, in a pinch all I had to do was stand up, and I'd have a few inches, well thirty to go before I broke the surface. Why couldn't I do it? Why couldn't I do what so many others could so easily do?

Before, I could fake it. I used the standby, the black girl's excuse, and sat near the shallow end swishing my legs. I'd pretend that the reason I didn't want to go all the way in was that I didn't want to ruin my fresh hairdo. But that day, I saw a girl with a perm go in and when she came out, she was whipping the hair out of her face. It didn't seem to bother her that kinks were forming by the millisecond. Maybe, it was time for her to re-touch or maybe, she just didn't give a darn. Since I now wore my hair in an afro, getting it wet was not devastating anymore, so I was out of even pseudo excuses.

Everyone could see I didn't straighten my hair anymore, so what was my concern for not diving in like all those boasters who went in needlessly head-first to the deep end. Did everyone there know that I was incompetent, that I swam like a stone?

Minute by minute, I grew more annoyed. Then my eyes went to someone who I really couldn't stand—the lifeguard. Every pool had at least one and while the instructors were in the swim, he (I'd seen guys perform this task) sat in his highchair, so dry, as he surveyed the situation. I knew first aid. I could do this job, well, most of this job. So far, I'd never seen any of them do anything besides stay poolside. Armed with just a whistle, I saw the blond-haired lifeguard with the flipped-up nose blow on a group who was play-dunking this other kid.

Whistle sound. Whistle sound. Whistle sound.

The trio was still horsing around, so the lifeguard climbed (finally) down from his perch, walked over to their area of the pool, and blew his whistle for the fourth time.

This time, they stopped immediately.

I could do that part of the job, easily, I thought. I was a great killjoy, just ask anyone who knew me.

I sighed and took a seat. In street clothes, dungarees

and a horizontal striped tee shirt, I was not allowed in the pool area and could only watch from behind a glass. Every now and then, I'd catch Tracy John's eye. He'd give me the fang face then return to practicing the Australian crawl or training for the 1980 Olympics or whatever they did in his advanced "fish" class.

"Didn't you feel like swimming today?" a lady asked. She was the only other guardian in this waiting area. The others went to a coffee shop or ran some quick errands during this time.

I looked at what was in the woman's lap: bright red yarn with two large needles.

Now, that was a good idea. She could finish a hat, some socks, and a scarf just in time for the fall chill if this was how she planned to use her free time.

"No, I didn't feel like swimming today. I think I'm coming down with a cold," I lied. I wasn't going into my hydrophobia (aquaphobia?) with a total stranger.

"Oh, well, then you are right not to go swimming. Wait till you feel better," she told me.

I nodded and watched her needle work. She was nimble, pearling fast. I preferred crochet to knitting because the snitching looked more flexible. In truth, I couldn't do either. I was good with gimp. Cissy, Millicent, and I used to spend every 6th grade recess gimping and talking. Despite the fact that practice makes perfect, I don't think there was much call for rubber sweaters.

I sighed (again). Maybe, I'll bring a book next time.

I'd get an Agatha Christie mystery from the library; that'd pass the time. I like the way she showed a safe murder, no gore or gruesomeness—just puzzle solving and propriety. I also liked the chic locale. I'd give anything to travel - I'd never been in a train or a plane or anything but I had an adventurous soul and I'd love to take an ocean liner out of the country way across the sea and stay there for twenty months to make up for this deficit.

-

The hour ended quickly enough I guess, in spite of my sour disposition. Tracy John emerged from the boy's locker room with his pickled skin reeking of chlorine. We exited the building and went down Lansdowne Avenue toward Greenway Street.

"Why don't you become a tadpole?" he asked me.

"Tadpole?" I asked and gave a big laugh. "What makes you think I would take beginner classes?"

"Because you can't swim," he said.

"How do you know I don't know how to swim?"

"You never go swimming with me or Leo."

"That doesn't mean I can't."

He stopped walking and grabbed my shirt. "So you can swim, Maine?"

"Of course not."

Tracy John made a face at me and asked, "Huh?"

I smiled; I loved messing with him. "Exactly!"

Chapter 5

Dinner was garlic catfish with way too much cayenne pepper for my taste, so I was stuck doing something I lovingly named after my vegetarian boyfriend. I 'pulled a Raymond' and ate around the main course trying to satisfy myself with the scalloped potatoes and the green beans.

Horace regaled us with stories from the (peacetime) front. He said how in the mess hall it was always: "Shut up! Eat up! Get Up!"

"I thought that was just during basic training. Why's everybody in a hurry now?" Leo asked.

"There's always another platoon waiting to get served."

"America should have more space," Tracy John said.

At that point, I zoned out. Horace had been home for a whole three days now and this was about the fiftieth chapter of The Tales of Private Upshaw I'd heard so far. If Horace wasn't telling us about military life, then he would go on and on and on about those pineapple drinks with rum. That, however, earned one of Ma's frowns since she discouraged alcohol consumption. I zoned back in at that point and almost jumped to my brother's defense, reasoning that it wasn't like he was a boy anymore, or even a teenager. He was a grown man living on his own miles and miles away from Dardon, PA. The United States Army thought he was responsible enough to entrust him with an M-16, various types of grenades, and even land artillery weapons. Why was Ma trying to deny him the right to have a cocktail if he wanted one?

Daddy sought to defuse the situation by saying, "Look at the bright side, Miss Sweet Thang. At least the Army got him to make his bed each day."

Horace grinned and reached for another roll.

More of that too seasoned fish was passed around, and I covered my plate.

The conversation then switched to the other short timer at the table, Leo. He was due to ship off to a special month-long tap dance intensive on Monday.

Leo described the grueling itinerary: wake up each morning at seven and dance until nine each night.

"That's too much dancing," Tracy John told Leo.

Daddy disagreed. He applauded the rigors of the schedule. He said, "Now, Tracy John, they had to separate the wheat from the chaff."

"When did you say the concert was?" Ma asked.

"July 30th," Leo said. He had everything relating to his upcoming nonstop dancing life memorized. Anyone could tell he was so looking forward to it. He didn't seem to have a dime's worth of doubt in this upcoming first extended stay away from home, but I wondered what it would be like without what he added to the family. I suppose I could always fill in and make a wisecrack at the end of every fifth sentence I heard like he did, but would that be the same? Only aggravating Leo could truly be aggravating Leo, right?

The light above the table flickered, and I got a flashback to the trauma of graduation. "Oh, no, here we go again," I said.

Daddy eyed the bulb with a sideway glance and shook his head. "That's down to its last hour. I'll change it after we finish eating."

"Don't worry, Maine, you won't be left in the dark like at your speech," Leo said, breaking up in jagged laughter despite his consoling words.

"I don't see what was so funny," I told Leo. "Do you know how hard I worked on that address that I wasn't able to give?"

"I'd be mad if I wrote a whole long talk, but couldn't say it," Tracy John said.

Leo took another bite of his catfish. "Maybe it was a blessing in disguise. Look at how bad Principal Abderholden was bombed. If that power outage was a little bit earlier, it would have let us out of our misery."

Ma used a napkin on her mouth. "Leo, your principal did a lovely job. He said exactly what he was supposed to say to young people. He talked about hope and change."

I rolled my eyes. "And change and hope."

"And hope that change changes hope's diapers," Leo said. Tracy John cracked up.

Ma gave them a stern look.

Horace shrugged. "He said the same boring thing at my graduation."

Daddy nodded. "They say that same thing at any graduation anywhere in this country."

"Yeah, and that was the problem," Leo said.

"My presentation was not boring," I said. "I was going to quote Aristotle and Plato."

Tracy John pulled at my sleeve. "What were you going to say about Play-doh?"

"Pla-to," I sounded out for him. "He was a classical philosopher and mathematician."

"I'd rather listen to clay," Leo said.

"The whole production had a sad tone to it, "Ma said. "I still can't believe they are shutting that school down and expecting our children to make do with a whole new space way over in another town. Those people don't want to accept us."

"God made this world for everyone," Daddy said. "No reason why we need to stay separate."

"They really don't want us there, Payton," Ma said.

"Not at all. Some of the people getting their heads knocked in those marches were white, Miss Sweet Thang."

Ma shook her head.

"I hope they don't have no fights like in Boston."

Horace asked, "What schools you know don't have

fights? Kids fight with other kids. That's how they do. Don't have to be black over white. It could be short against tall and fat against skinny."

"Yeah, but black white fights are the worst," Leo said.

A fight, a fight black against white. I wasn't an instigator, but I had to say this. "Yeah, maybe."

"God made this world for everyone," Daddy said again and repeated. "Some of the people getting their heads knocked in those marches were white."

Then he went on to say, "One thing for sure, we're all human beings and besides there should be no fighting whether no matter the color or the size or shape."

Still, I did ponder his solution.

Peace. Ah, Peace.

Daddy wastes his time here in Dardon. Ship him off to the Middle East peace summit.

Peace. Peace. Peace. That was his answer to everything.

Still, I wanted war because I was moved so far afield from my initial concern. Didn't anyone want to talk about my being valedictorian?

-

I generally like people. People of different races (though to be honest, aside from teachers, I didn't know anyone besides black people.) What the upcoming school year would be like.

"Be glad you didn't talk, Maine, your speech was

boring," Leo said.

"Leo, that's no way to speak to your sister," Daddy said. "And, Charmaine, just forget about what happened that night.Put it out of your mind."

"Yeah, black out the blackout," Leo said.

Daddy pointed at Leo with his fork. "Do you want to find yourself in the doghouse, young man?"

Leo held his bark.

"After supper, I would like to hear your talk, Charmaine. We all would," Daddy had a broad, warm smile said as if everyone was in favor of it.

Ma pleasantly nodded along, adding her support.

As for the rest of the Upshaws, a mutiny quickly ensued.

Tracy John turned to me. "Are we gonna have to listen to the whole speech, Maine?"

Horace looked down at his wristwatch. "I told Claude and them I'd meet them at seven."

Leo leaned on his elbow. "I'd rather change the light bulb."

Chapter 6

This was good news, but a complete surprise. I had placed my valedictorian speech in my top desk drawer, but I didn't think I'd have the occasion to utilize it ever again.

When I came downstairs, they were all assembled in the living room. Leo and Horace had claimed the couch, looking impatient already. Tracy John brought in his model car to occupy him. He rolled it across the carpet and offered me his divided attention. At least, Daddy was focused, even placing the custard dessert that Ma had set out for dessert to the side as he prepared to listen.

"Often in the annals of history –" I began.

"Wait a minute," Leo called out. "We heard this part."

"I've got to start from the beginning," I said.

"Why don't you start from the part where you thanked us," Horace said.

"I didn't write that part down. That was extemporaneous," I said.

"That was what now?" Horace said.

"I just made that part up when I was up there," I

said.

"Well, it was awfully nice," Ma said.

"Thank you, Ma," I rolled my shoulders back and gave it another try. "Often in the annals of history --"

Leo pointed at me wildly. "Is that the right word?"

I sighed. "Is what the right word?"

"Annals," Leo said, "I thought, annals meant -"

Horace elbowed him. "You're going to have us here all night."

Now, that was some defense. Daddy offered a better bluster by saying, "Leo, let your sister read her talk. Horace don't be in such a rush. Charmaine, continue."

I nodded. I looked dead at my brothers and said, "Of-ten in the an-nals of his-tory…"

They both groaned.

Tracy John laughed.

Now, Daddy gave me a stern look. I began again keeping my reading voice straight this time. It was then that the phone rang.

I stopped, but no one made a move to get it. Daddy made a gesture egging me to go on.

"Often …"

Ring.

"In the annals."

Ring.

"Of history."

Ring. Ring. Ring.

"Whoever it is, is awfully persistent," Ma said.

"I'll get it," Leo said.

Daddy stopped him. "We are in here to listen to your sister."

All of their eyes returned to me, but I folded the paper up.

"As soon as I start, the phone will go off again," I said.

"Whoever it was, gave up," Horace said.

I shook my head. "Oh, that's all right."

"Read the speech, Maine," Leo said, "You got five pairs of ears waiting."

"It's okay. Graduation is over. It's done with. I should do like you said and forget all my hard work and just move on," I said with a tug in my throat and a low head.

Next came a boast of "Aw, read what you have, Maine" and "Come on, Maine, read it."

I beamed. "Well, if y'all insist." I unfolded it and dove in. "Often…"

The phone rang again.

Daddy rose. "I better get that, Charmaine. I'll tell them to call back later."

Daddy was gone a few seconds before he returned with the command, "Horace, Leo. Come on with me?"

"What happened?" I asked.

"Can I come too, Unc?" Tracy John asked.

"A water pipe burst at your Uncle O's place. Tracy John, you stay here and take care of the women folk." Daddy told my brothers. "Come, you two."

Tracy John stamped his foot. "I want to see the

flood."

Daddy, Horace, and Leo left the house with the swiftness of firemen sliding down a pole.

Ma took Tracy John upstairs to get ready for bed and I heard Tracy John alternate between "Why can't I go to see all the water?" and "But I can swim!"

I went to my room, holding my speech like it was haunted. I was convinced that someone had put a spell on it when I wasn't looking. Why else would something bad happen to it each time I took it out?

Chapter 7

Around nine in the morning the thought hit me like a guided missile: If Uncle O's apartment was under water, where was he going to live? That's when I started to go into tremors and convulsions. Not another houseguest. Hadn't I danced that tune before? With Tracy John taking over my room when he first moved in with us. Then, with Uncle E when he was on the lamb.

When would it be time for a new number? It's not that I had anything against Uncle O. It wasn't like he had an obstinate disposition or had been to prison (on the other hand, he didn't have the face of an angel and he didn't know how to play the guitar). Nevertheless, if you asked me yesterday how I felt about Uncle O, I'd say I was neutral to him. He was just my relative. But today he'd climbed the charts on my oh-no-not-him list.

Periodically, from my window upstairs I checked to see if Daddy's station wagon was parked outside. When I saw the space was filled, I figured Daddy was at least back from being tied up at Uncle O's place.

Still, I stalled for another hour. I couldn't bring

myself to go downstairs. With time, my worst fears were confirmed. Curiosity got the best of me, and I braced myself. I drew on my intestinal fortitude. I thought there still might be a possibility. There still might be an ever so faint chance. So far, I haven't heard anything. *Be strong*, Maine. *Face your fears with courage.*

I slipped downstairs and stepped into the room wearing a tight smile.

Leo got up and downed me and said, "What's wrong with your face?"

I ignored his comment and moved deeper into the kitchen to get further into the brewing conversation.

Keep a positive attitude, Maine, *all is not lost. This was no time to give up the ship.* If I heard the words: "That ain't no way to treat family" from Daddy's lips, then I would know it was over. But, until that time, there was no need to freak.

Uncle O was in the center of things. He was shorter than both my daddy and my other uncle and he had a shiny, pie-face. He had on denim overalls and a painter's cap.

"It wasn't that bad, was it?" I asked them.

"Well," Horace said with a deep sigh. "Little things were floating."

"Like what?" I asked.

"Like the coffee table," Leo said.

Ma placed her hand to her chest. "Oh, my Lord,"

Daddy made a calming down motion with his

hands. "The important thing is that no one's hurt."

"You could say that again," Uncle O said.

"The important thing is – " Leo began.

Daddy shot him a look, and my younger brother clammed up.

"With all the confusion, you didn't have a chance to call your insurance. Why don't you give them a call now?" Daddy suggested to his middle brother.

"You think they're open on Saturday, Daddy?" Horace asked him.

"It's worth a try. Who are you with, Otis?" Daddy asked Uncle O.

Uncle O was mum, and I started to get that sinking feeling.

"What company are you with, Otis?" Daddy asked.

Again, Uncle O said nothing. It was obvious to me what was happening. He just sat there passively, looking into space, hoping the subject would change. How annoying! Just spit it out Uncle O, 'Nationwide isn't on your side'.

"Otis, you do have insurance, right?" Daddy asked.

"What's insurance?" Tracy John asked.

"It's all a big scam," Uncle O piped up. "The insurance people are betting that your house will be alright and you're betting that your house will cave in around your ears."

I rolled my eyes. That was some explanation. Not only was he a fully grown man with no foresight, but he lacked the patience to explain something so that his nephew could understand it. Why didn't Uncle O admit it? *He was not in good hands with Allstate.*

"Brother, please don't tell me what I think you're going to tell me," Daddy said. I could feel the disappointment in his voice.

Uncle O was only too happy to oblige and went quiet again.

I hung my head. *Unlike a good neighbor, State Farm wouldn't be there.* I might as well start boxing up my stuff right now to make space for him.

"Wouldn't the landlord be responsible for the accident?" Horace asked.

"I don't know. It depends," Daddy reasoned. "And even if he was, that would cover the property, not what's in it."

"And you just bought that nice green sofa," Ma said.

"Good thing you left the plastic on it," Leo said.

"Where are you gonna stay in the meantime, Uncle O?" Tracy John asked.

That's when I launched into my silent prayer of 'Dear God, I hate to bother you—' I made it that far when the doorbell rang.

It rang again. Since I was the closest, Daddy motioned for me to get it.

Reluctantly, I headed for the front door.

I opened it and saw the wide smiling face of my boyfriend Raymond. He bowed like Prince Charming.

"Good afternoon, Charmaine," he said, "Are you

and Tracy John ready for the program?"

Now, how did that slip my mind? I welcomed him in and offered him a seat on the living room couch and asked Raymond if he'd like something while he waited.

"No, thank you, Charmaine."

"Are you sure?"

"Yes."

"Are you positive?"

Raymond's eyes narrowed with concern. "Is everything all right, Maine?"

"Everything is fine," I said as I turned and walked into the wall.

"Charmaine!" he exclaimed.

"I'm fine. I'm fine," I said, holding my head. "Just give me a minute and I'll get my things and my cousin," I told Raymond.

I went back into the kitchen to check the result of the cliffhanger I'd left the room on. As I reentered the room, I saw that the powwow had broken up. All parties had dispersed and the only one left was Ma, getting a start on dinner by snapping string beans.

So, was pumpkin-headed Uncle O to bunk with us? Was I going to lose my room so soon after I had regained it? What did the future have in store? I couldn't bring myself to ask her. The words wouldn't come to my mouth. And what was the use anyway? I should be used to this by now. This thing is called life, and it's odd twists.

Chapter 8

William Shakespeare only made it to the sixth grade, but back in the 1600s, primary school, with their concentration on Latin and Greek, was super hard. How else could he have gone on to become the most celebrated playwright ever? In Clark Park, right off Baltimore Avenue, there was a production of one of his comedies, <u>A Midsummer's Night Dream</u>. It surprised me how broad the humor of this play was. The characters seemed to do everything short of slipping on a banana peel. The protagonist Nick Bottom appeared on stage wearing a donkey's face as a mask saying he'd "made an ass out" himself. He had been turned into this animal by the mischievous sprite, Puck—yeah, that old story. To further complicate things, Titania, the fairy queen, fell madly in love with Bottom, so continually you see this beautiful woman chasing a human jackass. Several times she even kissed this ass – I didn't know whether to laugh at this or cry. Meanwhile, there was also a character named Helena who was enthralled with a Demetrius (who, thankfully, did not remind me in speech or manner of the Demetrius I knew). Shakespeare's Demetrius was in love with another girl named Hermia but there was also a guy called Lysander who, due to the cross wires of magic, was taken by the other lady, Helena – I think. The second act ended, and I was lost. In a thick fog of romantic entanglements, I didn't fault the bard at all for my confusion. There was a lot of atmospheres with it being in the open air. Ducks honked. Birds scrambled.

A bee kept buzzing by me. When it came back around, butt first for the sting, I swung at it wildly. Then I got up, tripping on the blanket I'd spread out to cover the grass.

Tracy John laughed.

I stuck my tongue out to him.

Tracy John laughed harder.

I sat back down.

"Do bees fly south for the winter?" Tracy John asked.

"What do you think, Tracy John?" I asked. "They hibernate in caves like bears."

"Actually," Raymond said, "Bees don't migrate like birds do." He went into a detailed explanation of the short, tortured life of this species.

As he spoke, a gnat hung around my ears. At that point, I was about done with all this. That was another thing I hated about summer – all the darn nature. All the confounded outdoor activities. Who decided that being swarmed over was fun?

"It might be your perfume," Raymond guessed.

I nodded; I had used a little Bonnie Bell Pink Mist on my wrist and behind each ear for the occasion.

"That would explain why you two aren't under attack," I said. "I wish I could take a shower right here!"

Looking about I could tell I was in the minority; everyone else had hit a state of bliss wearing easy smiles to go with warm sunlight. Are people naturally happier in the summer? I wonder...

"Still upset about graduation?" Raymond guessed.

I sighed and tried to keep my upper lip stiff.

"Yes, she is," Tracy John said.

"Did I ask you to answer for me, Tracy John?" I asked him. "Besides, I have every right to still be upset. You work your finger to the bone, and what do you get?"

"Bony fingers," Tracy John answered.

I gave my cousin a fake strangle.

He wiggled away from my grasp.

"I wish they weren't closing down Dardon High. Who wants to take a bus to school?" I asked.

"We're not the only kids in America to be bused. Since the sixties, I bet a million kids have gone in to integrated schools," Raymond said.

"This is a whole lot of nothing. You know, if everybody looked the same, life would be easier," I said.

"How could you tell people apart?" Tracy John asked.

I pinched Tracy John's arm. "Maybe we could all

wear name tags."

"Or maybe people don't have to look exactly alike," Raymond said.

"See," I said. "That's where the problem starts; there's always going to be differences."

Raymond nodded. "A human being has a beating red heart and blue veins."

"I read that up until after World War II they used to segregate blood," I said.

"They still do that. If you get the wrong type of blood, it could kill you," Raymond said.

"I don't mean A positive and B negative. I'm talking black blood and white blood."

Tracy John tapped me on the arm. "Blood is red."

"Oh, I see what you're saying," Raymond said. "Yeah, that is a sad point in history."

"There are a lot of points like that in history," I said. "And, yes, Tracy John, blood is red."

"Actually, Tracy John, it's blue till it hits the air. And, Maine, I wouldn't worry about it," Raymond said and continued, "So what if it's a new school? You'll make it to the top again."

"I'm not going to make it again. Let someone else have a turn to have their monologue preempted by a blackout."

"Or a broken pipe," Tracy John said.

"What?" Raymond asked.

"We don't need to go into that, Tracy John," I told him which, of course, caused him to launch into:

"Maine was trying to give her speech last night to just us, but she couldn't because Uncle O's place flooded with water."

"Didn't I say that we didn't have to go into that?"

Tracy John showed Raymond how Leo was marked off by his thigh where the water at Uncle O's place had risen to.

"That would be up past my butt," Tracy John told Raymond.

"It was good you didn't go to help last night; you could have been swallowed up by the sea," I told Tracy John.

Tracy John turned to Raymond and said, "Did you know that Maine can't swim?"

Someone rang a bell to signal that the intermission was almost over.

Raymond went to get us something to drink.

"Why are you such a blabbermouth, Tracy John?"

Tracy John gave me that 'I'm innocent' look. "What did I say?"

"Just about everything, with your babbling."

"It's okay that you can't swim, Maine."

"What makes you think I'm still concerned with that?"

"You should learn how to swim, Maine. If you were in Uncle O's place, you'd still be under water."

"I don't want to hear about water, Tracy John."

"Okay, I won't bring it up anymore," he said.

I peered at him.I knew for things like this, I could

throw this little guy farther than I could trust him. He seemed to get far too much enjoyment out of making me wince.

Raymond brought back three varieties of sodas.

Tracy John grabbed the Dr. Pepper (The one I wanted.) I knew that Raymond liked straight Coca Cola, so that left me with an orange-colored thing. I flicked open the bottle cap and took a swig. At least, it was icy, and nothing is better when it's hot.

Another warning bell sounded telling all us theater lovers that the show was about to resume. I hunkered down for more of that guy with the (jack)ass face being mistaken for a dreamboat.

The couple next to us was eating a full meal. The smell of barbequed ribs kept hitting me.

The third act was even more frantic and was lost on me.

More bugs bugged me.

Maybe, it wasn't the elements that lowered my concentration level and distracted me from the program. I kept thinking about Uncle O, his soggy apartment, and his lack of insurance. If he moved in with us, I might as well construct a lawn sign and put it right at our address of 614 Dardon Avenue.

Memo to the world: Don't trouble yourself with premiums. When you've got someone like my daddy in your life, you have the best insurance plan in America. All your accidents are covered fully no matter who's at fault. No questions asked. No claims adjusters, no assessment.

Chapter 9

On our walk from the trolley, Raymond and I were long-limbed, slow-moving. My shrimp cousin was quick and bright running yards before us. There was still a lot of sunlight left for the day and he wanted to throw a few rounds of football outside with some of his friends.

Before leaving us, he did thank Raymond for as he put it 'letting him tag along'.

"It's always nice to have you. How did you like the show?" Raymond asked my cousin.

"I liked it pretty good," Tracy John said with a big smile. "It had too many words though."

"Well, that's not so bad. Remember what I said. Learn something new every day this summer. If your brain is not properly fed, it will starve to death," Raymond said.

I nodded along with my boyfriend's comment, but I knew that it was not true because some people had been emaciated of knowledge for years and walked around fine.

"Expect a full quiz from me when I get back from camp, Tracy John," Raymond said.

I frowned. "I wish you weren't going away, Raymond."

"Time will fly, Maine," Raymond said with his customary wide smile. "I'll be back before you know it."

"When you come back, the summer will be over. I don't want the time to fly," Tracy John told him and flitted away from us to his next activity.

Alone (together) now and standing before my yellow siding house, Raymond and I moved to the enclosed porch. We sat beside each other and looked longingly into each other. Raymond had wonderful eyes, very warm and wise, like that of someone far older than fourteen.

"All throughout the performance, Maine, I kept picturing you on stage. I could see you as the fairy queen."

I waved away his flattery. "I couldn't imagine trying to project my voice over the dogs barking and the cars whizzing by."

"Oh, come on. You have a great speaking voice. You'd be perfect for the stage."

"As interested as I was last term in being in movies, the thought of appearing on a live stage never appealed to me. It seems too much like work. Those people have to remember too many lines. I didn't think I could do that."

"For you, Maine," he quipped, taking my hand. "They'd rig a teleprompter."

"Oh, Raymond," I gushed.

I heard my Ma's voice. "Charmaine."

I ran to the front door. "Yes, Ma."

"Wouldn't you like to invite Raymond in?"

"No, Ma. Out here is fine."

"I have the fan on. It's nice and cool."

"Ma, we are fine out here," I told her and shut the door.

When I came back to Raymond, I took his hand and said, "I'm sure going to miss you over the next couple of weeks."

"Charmaine," Ma called to me from the door.

I rose once again and walked over to her, putting my hand on my hips. "What now?"

"Is that anyway in the world to answer me? And what are your hands doing in your imagination?"

I placed my arms down at my side.

"That's better. Would you two like something cool to drink?"

"No, thank you, Ma."

"Well, you can ask your friend?"

"Ma, will you please leave us alone?" I said as I stormed away from her.

"What's going on?" Raymond asked.

"Nothing urgent. She wants to know if we want lemonade or something."

"I guess this is what is known as Southern hospitality," Raymond figured.

"No, that's what's known as spying. She could get a job with the CIA."

He laughed.

"I'm serious, Raymond, look. We're responsible people, aren't we? We've never given her any cause to doubt our judgment. We're almost all senior high school students. We don't need a chaperone."

"Well, you never know when someone will decide to go wild and crazy."

I rolled my eyes. "Raymond, do you even know how to go wild and crazy?"

He nodded. "Yes, of course, but I think I'd have to do some research on it in the library."

That made me laugh. He was a nerd, but he knew he was a nerd – what's not to love about that?

"Let's make a pact," I said to him. "Let's promise to each do something totally off the wall this summer."

I watched his eyes glint at my suggestion.

"Deal?" I asked and held my hand out for us to shake it.

That's when he turned my palm over, opened it up, and kissed it, saying, "Deal."

Chapter 10

I peeked into Leo's room and saw him packing a suit-
case, lovingly wrapping his well scuffed tap shoes in
a white cloth.

"Need some help?" I asked.

Leo shook his head no. "I got it. You can carry it
downstairs for me if you want."

"Would you also like me to carry you?" I asked him.
"I always wanted to be a rickshaw."

Leo gave me a half smile and opened his sock
drawer.

"When are you going to start packing?" he asked.

I pointed to myself. "Me? What are you talking
about? I'm not going anywhere."

"That's what you think. You need to clear out for
Uncle O."

From the tone of Leo's voice, I couldn't tell if he was
dead serious or if he was picking with me. I stepped
closer to him. "What did you hear?"

He shrugged with a kind of practice nonchalance.
"Nothing, but you know how things go."

I stiffed my back. "Oh, what difference does it
make? I'm not the least bit concerned with that

anyway."

"Oh, sure," Leo said sarcastically.

"Oh, so you don't believe me?" I asked him, putting some steel on my back. "Well, let me tell you something, Leo. If Daddy decides to relocate fifty-seven of our uncles and one hundred and two of our cousins here, you wouldn't see me bat an eye."

He laughed. "If Daddy had that many relatives, Maine, you'd be sleeping on the roof."

Chapter 11

Where would I be in life when I wouldn't have to hand in argumentative essays or solve trigonomic equations? The answer was slowly beginning to surface. School prepared me for war (One battle after another battle. One test after test. Day in and day out I had to prove myself, constantly) but now that there was peace—I was lost. Last fall, I took two quizzes, had one presentation, turned in space, a project for science and three tests in one day. This summer, I had no crucibles, no deadlines – nothing. It was intense with all the many rivers I'd crossed.

This peace (the rest of my life) was vast. But now—I didn't know what to do with myself.

I had no plan. No structure. All I had was time, months of it; well, two and a half to be exact.

Why were half of June and all of July and August such long months filled with such long days? Why did it get dark at like 9 pm, what could fill up all that time with meaning, or even entertainment?

That afternoon, I mosseed about Dardon, all one and a quarter mile of it. I was accompanied by Millicent and Cissy. As they griped about their obligations, I did everything I could to not roll my eyes. *Oh, those lucky dogs with their nieces to watch and their band camps.*

Finally, I just went out and told them "I need a new life, guys."

"What's so wrong with your current one?" Millicent asked.

"Yeah, Maine, you're the valedictorian, why would you want to change anything?" Cissy asked.

'Because nothing lasts forever', I nearly sobbed out, but I cleared my throat to keep my voice sounding normal.

"That valedictorian stuff was June 12, 1976. It's now June 19th. It doesn't mean anything anymore," I said.

"Yes, it does. You got the highest grade in the whole class."

"For a school which they're tearing down," I said, "Don't you see? The clock is reset. I'll have to start all over again."

Cissy nodded. "You're right. You probably won't make it as high at William Penn Way."

"Why, because our new school won't be all black?" Millicent asked.

"Maybe that and maybe because they won't let you," Cissy said.

"But they can't, not if Maine comes up with the highest GPA."

"They like to keep things like that for themselves."

"It's going to be their space, their world. They

think everything they do is better. They think they're smarter. They think they have better hair."

Millicent said, "There's a difference between white and black hair really."

"Yeah, they try to get oil out of their hair, and we try to put grease in our hair," Cissy said.

"And they try to put curls in their hair and we try to get the kink out of our hair," Millicent said.

Right then, I had a hot comb flashback. The sizzle. The hiss. The crackling of hair as the heated comb till my hair laid flat instead of defying gravity my halo.

"I hope they don't make us listen to their music," Cissy said.

"Why would they make us listen to their music?" I asked.

"At school dances and stuff. Like during pep rallies and stuff. It's going to be wall to wall Led Zeppelin," Millicent said, pantomiming an air guitar solo.

"I hate head banging music," Cissy said, making a devil horn symbol with her right hand.

"I think that's sign language for 'I love you', Cissy," I said.

"How could it mean both?" Millicent asked.

"No, it's heavy metal. Rock on," Cissy said.

A common bit on sitcoms was to have a character try to act "black" and fail miserably because he or she was too white. I thought Cissy's disposition was just as awkward to the point of being painful to watch. Too black to parody "white" culture. "You are not pulling that off," I told her.

"And you know they are only going to elect themselves to stuff," Cissy said.

Millicent nodded. "There will never be a black president."

"Of the country?" I asked.

"No, of the student body. We can forget about running for anything because it's not going to happen. We just won't have the votes anymore to have things go our way. That's because that's way too out there," Cissy said. "That's like science fiction."

Chapter 12

Amidst the Holy Ghost sounds, after the scriptures were operated and between the twenty-minute testimonials, in church that Sunday, Rev. Clee turned an eye toward this being graduation season. He asked me to stand along with everyone else who was moving up.

Among the large hats, big scarves and crisp suits, four of us stood (Nadine Witherspoon and her twin brother Norman were going into primary school and Jesse L. Dickey got sprung from high school and me). People upped and down us and clapped; I gave a beauty queen wave and felt compelled to curtsey. I wondered if Rev. Clee would go one step further and call us out by name and perhaps mention (while he was at it) that I had earned the title of valedictorian.

But that dream was usurped.

As we soaked up the attention, PFC Upshaw took the chance to rise and say, "I ship in three days."

The spotlight shifted and the twins, Jesse, and I returned to our seats.

Thank you, Horace, for squashing my moment.

Chapter 13

Leo went first, then Horace. Horace was the hard one because Leo would be back for weekends. We wouldn't see Horace again for months.

Horace's plane left mid-day, so he didn't have an o dark thirty wake up.

Ma freshly pressed and let down the hem in his dress greens (when he first came home the blazer was too short in the wrist). I had to admit he looked pretty sharp for his send off; still, did anyone like goodbyes?

"That was the fastest eight days in history," I told Horace as we loaded up the station wagon.

"Yep," Tracy John agreed with me. "It was more like one. One minute."

"Do you miss us when you're in Hawaii?" I asked my brother.

"I don't know," he said, with a searching kind of sigh. "When I'm there, it's like here doesn't exist. When I'm here, it's like there doesn't exist."

I thought of his life here. He goofed off with Claude and the gang, played catch with Tracy John, and went out with his sometime girlfriend Robin. (Robin sure hadn't changed; she was what you call hopelessly devoted to Horace. She wrote to my brother during Basic Training and AIT with her fluffy bangs and high ponytail.) Last night, Ma made his favorite: beef tips and baked macaroni, like old times. So, his time in Dardon had no pressure. No urgency. No nothing. Who would want to leave this set up? Still, I was sure going AWOL had crossed his mind and Horace was giving me the answer he thought I'd like to hear. It's hard to choose between two lives, even if one was undemanding.

"Horace knows that his hometown experience is over," Daddy said. "He's a man about it."

Horace nodded. "One thing's for sure you can't go backwards. You can only go forward."

Frowning deeper, I didn't mind when Daddy was right but I hated it when Horace was. What happened to Horace-the-screw-up? That fun loving guy that only last October got caught stealing the hubcaps, where was he? Why was he now so serious and thoughtful? Had the army training he'd gone through put him in a permanent military mind?

Philadelphia International Airport was not a far drive so after about twenty minutes we were there in the snaking labyrinth of lanes. The options seemed endless. I didn't know there were so many airlines. They had names like United and Frontier.

Horace checked in his duffle bag, and we took the escalator upstairs. There, there was an entire shopping center which I would have loved to tour, but Ma (overprotective) told me not to. Nervously, she said we had to stay together. What were we in some foreign country all of a sudden? I was fourteen years old – it wasn't going to get lost. Even if I did, I could have found my way to gate 21C by myself. But I wasn't allowed to. Like rice sticking together in a pot, we all made it to gate 21C – together.

Of course, we were way early. I watched as the arrivals gate became departure. I watched the men in orange vests rush in. They cleaned and fueled the plane.

"Give us a call as soon as you get to a pay phone," Ma told him, already crying and wiping her eyes with a Kleenex.

"I will, Ma," Horace promised.

More delays.

Horace chased Tracy John around the rows of armless chairs in the waiting area then over by empty rocking chairs that faced the big windows. They were getting so wild with their laughing and horsing around a few people turned and stared but just to notice, no one seemed bothered.

At last, it was time to board and Horace didn't have to wait. They asked for members of the armed services to board first. They called the row of seats that Horace was in, and all the fun was over.

He gave us hugs one by one and told us all to take care of ourselves.

With a bus or a train, you could run quickly and

go to the window and wave till the vehicle pulled away. But, after Horace entered the plane's door, he disappeared.

Still, mom kept waving.

I've never been on a plane, but I can imagine what it's like sitting in a window or aisle seat buckled up tight while the captain prepares for flight and covers miles in seconds high above the clouds. It must feel like freedom.

"Well, I guess, that's that," Daddy said.

That was when Tracy John broke his stoic seven-year-old routine. It was so plain to see in his suddenly lonely eyes and the way his lips hung down.

We went to the floor to ceiling windows and Tracy John's neck stretched and stretched as he watched the aircraft take off hot into the sky.

-

During the ride home, conversations were slow in coming.

Daddy wore his customary wide smile and tried to keep our spirits up. "People go and they come back."

"And then they go again," Tracy John said.

"And then they come back again," Daddy said.

Chapter Fourteen

I'd seen him before; he was missing his right leg. His left had been amputated over the knee.

After getting out of his wheelchair, he sat by the water with one hand in it. Without using the ladder, he hoisted himself in. With some adaptation, he seemed fine. He swam a choppy crawl, breathing either with every stroke or every fourth stroke. I wondered if he was counting somewhere well in the back of his mind.

"Still don't feel like swimming today?" the knitter asked as she joined me in the waiting area.

I looked at what was in the woman's lap this time: neon green yarn with her two large needles. She was on the verge of finishing a hat, some socks, and a scarf in time for the fall chill if this was how she used her free time.

"No, I—" began then drifted off.

She didn't seem to notice because she pointed at the injured man. "Look at him. Isn't that amazing?"

I nodded and watched the man. He was nimble, his fast strokes slicing fast though the water.

Then he had the nerve to flip on his back and kept going.

She shook her head. "Oh, that poor man."

Poor man? What was she talking about? There was nothing pitiable about him. He could swim. As far as I was concerned, he was another showoff.

I turned my gaze back to Tracy John and his friends.

Once again, they were horsing around, so the lifeguard climbed down from his perch, walked over to their area of the pool, and blew his whistle for the first then second time.

This time, they stopped.

I could do that, I thought. I still couldn't swim but I was a great killjoy, just ask anyone who knew me. I'd love to have a job like that, instead of murdering time, escorting my cousin to things and waiting while he was doing the Australian crawl or training for the 1980s Olympics or whatever they did in his advanced fish class.

I thought of the rest of my day, but all I could wait for was a letter from Raymond by the end of the week since there was a three-day lag.

That made maybe five letters I'd sent him and not got one back. *What gives?*

That was it. I was going to learn to swim. But I had to learn how to swim my way. Using the strength that had always pulled me through, I thought of taking a book out from the library. *I was* so good at absorbing material—that was all I had to do, skim a few pages and I'd get it down. I'd be zipping across lakes.

I never really looked into anything. *I didn't* have any interest *straight A's* in everything means I have an aptitude for everything, wet or dry.

I sighed and took a seat. In street clothes, dungarees, and a horizontal striped tee shirt, I was not allowed in the pool area and could only watch from behind a glass, as always. Every now and then, when I caught Tracy John's eye, he'd give me the fang face and I'd give him one back as if to say, mock me today but soon all things will be equal, or maybe since I was such a fast study, I could get superior. The sooner I read up on it – the sooner It would be done.

Chapter 15

After swimming, I took a still dripping Tracy John to the library which was located up Long Acre Boulevard right next to St. Joseph's Nursery School.

I tried the front door of the library only to find no give. I tried again. Then again. Still, it didn't open.

"Look," Tracy John said.

I finally did. The sign said:

> *Closed due to renovation.*
> *Sorry for the inconvenience.*

"What does that and that word mean?" Tracy John asked, pointing to the long words posted.

I shook my head. "They're gonna fix it up for the whole summer. I'll be damned."

Tracy John smiled devilishly. "Ohhhhhhhhhh, you cussing."

-

Let down again, I stomped home fuming. I was all too ready to break out a lounge chair (really, all I had was an armchair, but I pretended) and soak up some sunshine with a new book in hand.

How often can my original summer plans be dampered? All I wanted was to take out a new book or two (or twenty). I wanted some fun, a way to escape and have adventure, heck, I'd even settle for the opportunity to learn something.

This was maddening, all it was over and over. Ready? Set? Zip. Or, as Horace told me the army put it: "hurry up and wait." Was this what life was like? A lot of sizzles and no steak?

Ma was there to greet Tracy John and I as we got back home. She had on her apron and told us we were in time to help her shuck the corn—like that was an activity no one was looking forward to.

"Are we gonna have a cookout?" Tracy John asked.

(I hoped not. I hated grilled food with lines on them.)

Ma nodded and pinched Tracy John on the cheek. "With nice weather like this, it would be a shame not to."

I rolled my eyes. 'Nice' weather was about all that summer was good for. Beautiful summer days. It's always lovely outside. Summer rhymes with bummer and that's all it was, no matter how it was dressed up.

Finally, I blurted out "Cookouts – I think they should be against the law for smoking."

"What foolishness is coming out of your mouth, Charmaine?" Ma asked.

I moved over to the table and looked through the pile of mail.

"Leave that alone, Maine. I'll tell you when you have something.... from Raymond."

"Can I do anything in this house?" I asked.

"Yes, you can get your hands off your imagination," she told me.

Tracy John ran up beside me and eagerly shuffled through the letters, making a scattered mess of things. I eyed Ma just to affirm the obvious, she would never correct, the precious one, him. He pulled out a post-card with palm trees on it. "The one's from Horace."

I used my pointer finger to make circles in the air. "Whoopee."

"Maine, you're 'bout to be on thin ice --" Ma began.

"Maine is mad because the library is—What's the word?" Tracy John looked at me to fill in.

I sighed. "It's renovated. They are sorry for the inconvenience. Blah, blah, blah."

"Well, it's that lovely." Ma clapped her hands together. "Everything will be all shiny and new when it opens again."

"And Maine cursed." Tracy John blurted out.

Ma shot me a look and the room got ponderous. I mouthed to Tracy John, "I'm going to kill you."

"Maine, shame, shame shame," Ma said, handing me a handful of ears. "You better get to shucking."

Before I knew it, I was surrounded by tassels and husks, breaking the stems. All of this to prepare for what? Some dogs gone striped food.

"Is this enough corn?" I asked my mom.

She didn't answer. She and Tracy John had moved on to spearing cherry tomatoes and green peppers on the shish kabob stick.

I took this opportunity to sneak away to my room. Once there I found the five books I owed to that now closed library and threw them on my bed, not caring whether the special binding could take the impact. On average, I read things two and a half times before I return them anyway (once to get the gist of the story, twice to go through the whole ride again and the last half times when I hit the juicy parts).

I couldn't re-read these books for a fourth time. I just couldn't. This was horrible. These circumstances that I'd found myself in had even stopped me from being a nerd.

-

Now, something was burning or rather grilling. I peeked out the one window in my room and looked down. Everything was flipped as far as gender roles. Dad stood over the raging flames holding a cooking utensil for a change, and Ma went to the side chatting with Mrs. Whitaker, not participating in this stage of the meal preparation at all.

Yep, it was on.

By the time I made it downstairs every inch of the back yard was filled. People were sitting on folding chairs, kitchen chairs, dining room chairs, and stools.

I wanted to inform everyone. What was this all

about, some pre-Independence Day shin dig? When the Declaration of Independence was signed, many Black people were still enslaved, so we should celebrate? It was useless as a holiday.

Besides, nothing competes with Christmas gifts.

Valentine's day has candy – dark chocolate candy in heart shaped boxes to die for. Independence Day weekend has these cookouts where you get hot dogs with lines on them and fireworks. Frederick Douglass's speech that he gave on the fifth of July. And what difference does this holiday mean? We already had the day off.

And don't get me started on Flag Day. It doesn't even have fireworks.

I grabbed a glass of lemonade and made my way to Uncle E. He was all about music.

He was kind of Zen with it. Playing the guitar and singing as a kind of therapy and he had a bunch of neighbors amassed around him for the session.

As long as they stayed on beat, Uncle E could carry about any rag tag group. There was a pureness to his vocals, with a tenor as smooth as melted butter. Clarity. Effortlessly, he hit each note with precision, yet he somehow remained spontaneous.

Never have I heard such fabulous music accompanied by makeshift instruments: a ceramic toy horse (half filled with dry beans so it works like a maraca) Tracy John shook that, most did plain old clapping hands, still Mr. Jones and an intricate use of salad tongs.

One guy just snapped his fingers.

Just when I thought it was over, the guys gave an acapella encore.

I guess I could have joined in with a spoon.

I was glad that I had gotten out. Being in the open air made everything felt better. My neck joints melt loose. Synovial fluids flowed freely.

Oh, how summer irked me.

Chapter 16

It'd been three weeks.

It'd been four weeks.

It'd been five weeks since I'd heard from Raymond—but who's counting...

Finally, I was able to catch my two best friends while they were back in town. When they came over, I spent the entire time telling them how much I missed Raymond.

"Why do you think I haven't gotten a letter from Raymond? I thought he really cared about me. How could I have confused his sincerity? I thought he was true blue," I said.

"He is nice, and he does care about you, Maine," Millicent said.

"Maybe, he didn't bring any stamps," Cissy said.

"Oh, come on," I said.

"Yeah, and the camp that he's at is so remote that he can't get to the post office."

"Maybe Spider-man --" Tracy John began, then corrected himself. "Maybe Raymond has the stamps but didn't mail them because he forgot where all the mailboxes were."

"Maybe he was thrown from a horse on his head and all his bones are broken," Cissy supposed.

I frowned. "Well, at least that would be closure."

"He'd be in intensive care," Cissy said. "That's harsh."

I nodded. "But he'd be all better by September."

That night I still fumed. Raymond is probably somewhere reading in a tent, I suppose reading with a flashlight was easier to navigate instead of writing to me. He seemed like he really cared. The last time I saw him, he kissed my hand. Maybe it wasn't a kiss. Maybe that was some sort of kissoff. Maybe, that was why he hadn't written.

But, my boyfriend had forgotten about me.

He was always so kind and thoughtful. Time flew when I was with him, and we never ran out of things to talk about.

I missed him like I missed school. Time galloped at school. It seemed like as soon as one period started one would end.

Now, each lazy, hazy day of summer was like 1000 years. There was no one to hang out with on a consistent basis. Everyone was scattered to the four winds doing their hobbies and activities. It was easier to stay close to people when it was mandatory that you saw them seven hours a day.

School...

Raymond...

You think you have something in your life, and it

flows through your hands like water.

My eyes welled up and tears tumbled down my cheeks.

That night, I gave up writing to Raymond, but I still had all the pencils, ink, erasers, markers, pens, and drawing tablets left from school and the burning desire to record my daily observation. I went to my desk and pulled out my blank diary.

I composed the following:

Today was not good. Hope tomorrow is better.

P.S. I need to be more detailed if this diary thing is going to work out.

Chapter 17

There wasn't too much trade and industry in Dardon, PA. Just a pizza place, a deli, two banks, and way on the other side of my one-mile sized town, there was a Donut World. As luck would have it, I found what I wanted there. To be exact I saw a Help Wanted sign in the window. I rushed up to it like it was a geyser. I got close to it and let the stream of opportunity run all over me.

These donuts were the dense cake variety, the yeasted ones in the shape of a ring that dissolve as you chew, and then there are filled donuts with a variety of fruit or cream fillings.

"Would you like one?" the owner asked. Like my mom, he seemed to have a definite southern accent.

I nodded eagerly. "Yes."

"How many?"

I laughed, "Just one."

He bagged up a donut and handed it to me. "That will be fifteen cents."

"Oh, no. I'm here for the job."

"Oh," he said, all business, with tongs he removed the dessert from the paper bag and put it back with the display.

He up and downed me and went to the drawer pulling out a form. "Here's an application. You're sixteen, right?"

I shook my head. "No."

"Do you have working papers?" he asked but before I could answer his question, he gave me the ultimatum. "If you bring in your papers, you can work."

Walking back home, I muddled over what had just happened: What color was my parachute? Donut World. This would be a perfect way to do something this summer. All I would need now is for my mom or dad to sign off.

-

Ma spread the clothes on the line to dry going into her apron pocket for clothespins.

I asked her if I could be an adult.

"You gotta be kidding, Honey."

"No, Ma, I'm serious, I want to work with donuts."

"Are you really fixing to deal with, what's the word, irate customers?"

"There won't be any, Ma. Everyone likes donuts."

"People are liable to wig out about anything. Don't matter what the product is. You don't want somebody in your face complaining. Nope. It's not a good idea. I'm not for it, Charmaine."

"I can handle it, Ma. I'm not a baby, for Christ sake--"

"Don't use Jesus's name," Ma warned.

I closed my eyes to center myself as I said, "For Pete's sake, then. I'm fifteen years old!"

"Didn't I tell you; I didn't want you to be a teenager this summer," Ma said. She handed me an end of the one sheet and pointed to the far end of the line. I stretched the fabric, simmering.

"I'm not a baby, Ma. Soon, I'll be able to get a job without you saying so."

"But until then you need my signature if you want to work there," Ma said. "Maine, put it out of your mind."

"But it's my life. It's my life," I said. "This is unreal. You two are being unreasonable. There's nothing wrong with me having a job."

"You're not getting a job, Maine, and that's the end of it," Ma said.

"This is unreal." I threw up my hands. "And unfair. I'm going to be selling donuts. I don't think I'll need a hard hat. No one was wearing goggles or even gloves. All I have to do is play with the flour with my bare hands. It's not like I'm coal mining, where's the danger?"

"Charmaine, that shop is in a bad spot by the creek there. And, you'll be handling money, making change. I'm sorry, Maine, no. You're not ready for it."

"Ready for it? But I was valedictorian."

"Charmaine, that's about enough on the matter."

"Well, I'll see what Daddy has to say."

"I think you will find us of one mind about this, Maine."

"How do you know?"

"Cuz, I'm a mind reader."

Chapter 18

It was hopeless. There was no repair, no escape—
between June 22nd and Labor Day was going to be
sheer Hell.

Of course, Daddy took Ma's side, but at least he
softened the letdown. He asked about the donut store
hours - nothing past dark because donuts don't like
the dark. He asked who I would be working with
(Donut people, of course.)

Finally, he asked, "Why do you want a job anyway?"

No, that question answered itself. I had nothing to
do. I wanted something to do. I had to hand it to hobbies. I didn't have any distractions.

And, he let me make my closing summation. "As
well as the benefits, I would like to have a job. I would
like to learn how to manage money and build life
skills. And grow. As a person."

I always thought of my father as having a kind
face, blunt and big features but kind and understand-
ingly arranged. It always gave me a glimmer of hope
at times like this.

"I'm sorry, Maine. No."

Chapter 19

The loopy theme music of the <u>Dick Van Dyke Show</u> ended and a brand of humor, so dippy, so zany followed. It wasn't really my thing, but it beat my other choices: soap operas and game shows. Summer had taught me one thing, the network TV and UHF that looked so intriguing on an occasional day off during the school year became a bore if watched with any regularity.

Why, oh why, do they call it commencement when everything is over?

And, moreover, I still didn't know how I was going to fill all the days. Start the recommended summer reading list? Before August? Even I wasn't that much of a geek.

Tracy John came in and plunked himself down beside me.

"It's time for my swim class," he said.

"Ask Ma to take you," I told him.

"Why can't you? You're not busy."

I rolled my eyes. "Tracy John, do you know what the word tact means?"

"No."

"Well, one day you will and then maybe you'll learn

to use a feather instead of a hammer."

He rolled his eyes. "That doesn't sound like any fun."

I tried to give his shrimpy neck a fake strangle, but he wiggled out too quickly.

"Maine are you going to sign up to be a tadpole?" he asked.

"For the millionth time," I began, keeping in mind that it's not a good idea to yell at children. "NOOOOOOOOO!"

Tracy John eyebrows shot up at my scream and said, "You are a weirdo."

Then Ma came in and let me have it with her 'you know better than to raise your voice in this house'. She made me turn off the television and she gave me two minutes to get ready to bring Tracy John to the Y.

-

The sky was a cloudy gray, yet looking up gave me the idea. As I walked holding my cousin's hand, I knew what I would do when I got to the pool where all the showoffs were. How did the saying go if you can't beat them join them? That was what I'd do.

I could write to Raymond that night and tell him how I was stepping out of my comfort zone finally. I've seen people swim enough in my life. So, why couldn't I?

So, what if I wasn't trained? Someone had to be the first. You can't tell me that the caveman (or woman) happened upon a pond and didn't dive in because they hadn't taken lessons at the YMCA. There was something to be said for on-the-job training.

I would prove to the world that I was no scaredy cat.

The heavy chlorine smell hit me as we reached the parking lot. Once inside, while Tracy John was changing, my plot began to unfold.

I strode to the edge of the pool.

Have no fear. Have confidence.

Before going in, I could imagine myself in there taking a deep breath, floating, then treading in water. (Can't anyone do that?) Wouldn't it just be so natural?

Then I got bolder. *Breathe Maine. Come on in and out. In then out.*

Swim.

I was going to swim, doggone it. I was going to glide through the water like it was air. I was going to put dolphins to shame with how well I was cutting through the blue.

I believe I can swim.

I wasn't going to be shown up any longer.

I kicked off my sandals.

I peeled off my top shirt, so I only had a tank top and shorts on.

I can swim. I can swim.

Splash.

So far so good.

Then I sank.

Not so good…

Chapter 20

The water refracted the sound of screams. The panic suspended in midair. There was no such thing as drowning with dignity, and moreover that was not my goal. I really thought I could somehow swim.

All the time that I spent submerged went by in a snap.

When a lifeguard saw me, he performed an emergency rescue.

Then there was me.

Swimmers (and I use that term loosely, who are taking in water while attempting to stay at the surface), lifeguards look at swimmers in this condition by looking for arms flailing vertically, with the body vertical and no supporting kick. Swimmers who have become tired and are having trouble swimming (distressed swimmer) and may or may not be calling out for help.

Swimmers who are inactive in the water, or otherwise were passive drowning victims, weren't that hard to corral. The lifeguard could have put me on the rubber raft or put out the gigantic lifesaver or the rope, the help rope.

During my voyage to the bottom of the pool, the watery sound of voices faded, mystifying the weirdest thing that went worming through my mind. "ALL SWIMMERS MUST TAKE A SHOWER BEFORE USING THE POOL."

You must get wet before getting wet. Huh?

I swallowed a couple gallons of chlorine before I was yanked up to the surface. Then I was thrown to the curb of the pool.

Someone screamed, "Maine!"

I coughed and coughed.

Everyone sat hunched over me. Yelling and directing me. "Breathe normal" and "Take a deep breath."

Someone had the nerve to shout, "Relax."

Relax?

I hacked and waved my arms. I had almost died. I looked about wildly.

Black, brown, and beige faces but at the center one white one, the lifeguard.

My eyes stung, but I was safe on dry land.

Chapter 21

Ma had me cut the cabbage into quarters. "Take off those wilted leaves," she told me.

I kept my head down, somber. Ma had gotten the briefing but seemed not to dwell on it. As I cut from core of the cabbage and took off the discolored pieces, I half expected to escape scot free.

The bacon fried until crisp. Ma put the strips into paper towels to drain.

Ma crumbled the cooked bacon into the cabbage.

"Maine, not everyone was meant to swim," she told me.

I had a feeling she would tell me that, even if I were born a guppy. I felt relief because of the sermon.

Dinner served Uncle O over opened the floodgates. "Maine, that was a pretty stupid thing to do."

I nodded, knowing that I was now taking lectures from my wayward uncle.

"Yeah, Maine, stupid," Tracy John said.

As tempted as I was to tell Uncle O, 'why don't you go back to your soggy apartment?' but I kept my mouth sealed.

"What is your reason, Maine?" Ma asked me.

"I thought it would kick in," I said.

"What would kick in?" Uncle O asked.

"Knowing how to swim," I muttered.

"How is knowing how to swim going to kick in if you don't know how to swim?" Uncle O asked.

I shrugged. "Instinct."

Tracy John burst out laughing and said, "You stink, Maine."

I rolled my eyes. "Every human being has the innate ability to swim. It's as natural as breathing. I stood and pointed to my chest. "It's within us."

Daddy's hand raised to the sky as if he was trying to restrain himself by summoning up Jesus himself to calm him. When he finally spoke, he said these words that shook the room. "If you don't know how to swim, Charmaine, STAY OUT OF THE POOL!"

I could feel the ground shake from his words, as I returned to my seat. Everyone was quiet for a beat or two.

In her attempt to smooth over the situation, Ma said, "She seems like she's all right, Peyton. Maybe that's enough discussion about this."

"I know this girl right here," he pointed at me. "I know she has good sense not to jump into a pool of water knowing she can't swim."

I was about to tell him all about how I was going to get a learn how to swim book from the library but the library was closed for renovations for the entire summer. I also wanted to tell him that I was bored carting

Tracy John around and while I was at it I wanted to tell him I was sick of watching those show off swimmers and more importantly my boyfriend, Raymond, promised me he cared about me, he promised, he vowed that he would write and not forget about me, but he did. I hadn't gotten anything from him; forget about one letter, I hadn't gotten one syllable.

I started to tell my father all of this, but I stopped myself. Because I knew there was no excuse possible that would suffice with his sky-high standards. I was in control of my actions, so I could offer a defense. I jumped in; I wasn't pushed.

But what did that mean? Was I crazy? I wish I was rich because rich people are never crazy—they're eccentric. But okay. I'll own it, to jump into a swimming pool without skills—Insane? Maybe. Okay, definitely.

In the history of the world how many people did what I did? Probably, just me.

It was hours after the incident, and I could smell chlorine constantly. I wondered when that would stop.

Maybe, it was a permanent condition. I wasn't referring to my soggy lungs. This nuttiness.

All that water had no effect on my afro. In fact soaking up the moisture added glisten.

Hours after this episode, my skin itched from dryness.

Nevertheless, swimming (if you could call that experience that I had) made my skin dry as a lizard.

I fell into a big bowl of cold blue broth, which

amounted to a dip in the pool like gravy biscuits.

My pulse was normal.

My brain waves, normal.

My oxygen flow is (I guess) normal.

Did I need to be monitored?

As I went down for the count with no skill, I had no plan to climb to the surface.

A person could theoretically have an infinitesimal amount of near-death experiences in one's lifetime.

"Okay, I learned my lesson," I announced it to the table.

"You will never enter a pool again, Maine?" my cousin asked.

"Tracy John, I'm not even going to join a carpool."

Chapter 22

Falling kills more people than drowning. But, falling was more of a danger for older people, as water deaths struck younger people. Sadly, toddlers were especially susceptible to these sorts of accidents. Yet, every avid swimmer I ever knew claims that they were 'born' swimming. So, what was the right way, it seemed you're damned if you do (make sure you're giving your child a rich exposure to aquatics) and damned if you don't (avoid water 100%).

I thought of the unfortunate/fortunate life of Matthew Webb. I read a book about him during self-sustained silent reading last year. He was the first person to swim the English Channel. It was almost 40 miles, which is like 400 streets. It took him hours and hours, like nearly a day, but he did it. He was a champion, a professional swimmer—arguably the best in the world. And what did he do for an encore: he drowned. Yep, as ironic as that may sound, despite his expertise and international adulation, he went down. He continued with these "stunts', marathon swimming everywhere about the globe, and he died on his quest to swim in something called the

Whirlpool Rapids (yeah, I bet that sounded real safe).

Does any of this make any sense, that a world class swimmer could drown? It all led me to the conclusion that water was the most powerful force on earth, stronger and more unpredictable than fire even. It will have you believe it's there to be shaped and controlled, but it lords over us, taking up two thirds of the world. The fact that we knew less about the bottom of the ocean than we know about outer space was frightening. Neil Armstrong, Buzz Aldrin, and Michael Collins were all going the wrong direction, they should have taken our flag down several leagues. The real mysteries were beyond our shores.

The next day, I was back at the Y with my regular clothing: a tee shirt and cutoffs. Underneath, I had a bathing suit, a bright color block one-piece (The stretch-infused fabric ensured comfortable movement). I wore this to face out.

Tracy John's swim trunks resembled denim shorts. He separated from me as soon as we walked in the door and that stench of chlorine assaulted my nostrils.

Tracy John ran off to be with his fellow show offs around the pool side.

By this point, I had had it with the knitting woman I always ran into, so I opted to wait outside by the parking a lot.

Philadelphia got the worst of all worlds: harsh winter winds and sweltering summer heat, but that day wasn't half bad.

I took a space below the sky and under a tree and vegged. For once I was glad that I hadn't brought anything to read because it was nice to exist and still my inner turmoil. I closed my eyes and mimicked what little I knew about transcendental meditation. Crossing my legs was easy, but the introspection was difficult. I still didn't know why I took the leap. What was I looking to gain? What did I really think was going to happen? I wasn't the reckless type. I wasn't wild or crazy (Though I had promised Raymond I would do something). I didn't have an answer. It was like I was possessed. The water looked so welcoming, so inviting. Was it possible that I had been seduced even though I knew I couldn't swim a single stroke?

I opened my eyes back up when the lifeguard arrived.

He passed, throwing me a smile then a double take.

"Hey, aren't you the one?"

I would have loved to have ducked him, but he was standing right before me. "The one?" I asked, still trying to play it off.

"Yesterday, didn't I have to pull you out?" I flinched as he continued with his recollection. "You're the one who went under, right?"

I nodded slowly, reluctantly, embarrassedly. I unscrambled my legs and rose to my feet. "I never thanked you properly. Thank you."

"No need. It's my job. I'm glad I got a chance to do

it."

He sounded excited. His Adam's Apple was jogging in his throat when he spoke.

I know it's thyroids and cartilage, but I was fascinated.

Beyond that, he did appear altered today.

His lank hair grew darker when wet. In the open air it was a distinct shade of light blond and free flowing. I had to do a double take.

"Well, thank you --"

"I'm Leif."

"Leif? How do you spell that?" I blurted out. It always bothered me when I didn't know things.

His brows knitted together for a moment but then he obliged. "L-e-i-f."

"Your name is life with the letters mixed up."

He laughed. "I guess."

"And you became a lifeguard."

He laughed again. "I guess... So, you don't know how to swim. You never learned?"

"I don't want to be a tadpole."

"You won't be an actual tadpole. That's just a goofy label they use here."

"Well, whatever they call it. I don't want to be a beginner; I'd feel like a baby. I'm going into 10th grade."

"I'll be in 11th grade."

"And, you can swim. I bet really fast, probably like Mark Spitz."

"Nope."

"Nope? You were never interested in the 100 meter or the 200 meters?"

"Nope," he repeated.

"Then why do you work at a pool?"

"To do what I did the other day with you. God, that was a crazy rush, so much better than practice. I didn't think I'd ever get the chance to do it in real life."

Odd. I would think that's what intrigued me about the job, so he became a lifeguard to be a lifesaver (not like the candy).

"Saving a human life has always been my dream."

I nodded slowly. "You're welcome?"

Later as the session ended, I went back in to get Tracy John. I saw Leif performing one of his other tasks, testing the pH of the water.

When Leif saw me, he said, "Hey. What high school are you going to?"

Tracy John elbowed me. "Maine, the lifeguard is talking to you."

I turned to him only to find up close how a row of pale freckles felt about his nose. That happens to some fair skinned people as a reaction to summer. After the heat subsided, so would this smattering of melanized cells. "I'm going to William Penn Way in September."

"Oh, yeah, they changed our name," he said, once again with that breeziness, that ease. With a wave, he made his way back to the big chair and took a seat upon its lifeguard throne.

When my thoughts returned to Tracy John, his

copper-colored eyes seared into me.

I returned the rude glare to him, and he turned away but then he came back. In fact, Tracy John looked at me strangely the whole way home, but I didn't worry about it at first because he always had something cooking. Always very energetic with those penny-colored eyes took up the pupil and most of the eye socket space.

But then after two blocks, he was still giving me the freeze out, this scorn. Finally, I asked him, "What the heck is wrong with you?"

He pointed his finger at me. "Maine, you can't dump Raymond."

"What?"

"That lifeguard who saved you."

"Yes."

"Stop talking to him."

"Huh? Why?"

"Because you shouldn't talk to him."

"Why not?"

He swiveled his neck. "Why do you think, sister?"

"Tracy John, do you know everyone in this world?"

"No."

"Well, then don't be prejudiced."

"I'm not being prejudiced. I'm standing up for my friend, Raymond."

"Raymond is not my boyfriend anymore."

Now, Tracy John's eyes were the size of half dollars. "Since when?"

Real steady support from this one.

"Since I haven't gotten a single letter."

"So?"

"I'm done with him if he's done with me. I'm not going to just hold on."

"Why can't you?"

"Tracy John, you're seven years old. You don't know anything about anything."

"I know that lifeguard saved your life with the help of the rest of us. But don't dump Raymond. It's not his fault the mail is slow."

"There's nothing wrong with the post office. It's him."

"But you don't know that for a fact."

"I don't want to talk to you about this."

"I'm saying don't give up on Raymond. He's much better, he's seen all the Twilight Zones and he knows all about dinosaurs. And we went fishing that time."

"That sounds really important."

Tracy John stomped his foot. "It is."

"Maybe Leif, the lifeguard could be my summer boyfriend and Spiderman could be my boyfriend when I go back to school," I managed to say to my little cousin before a derisive laugh escaped my lips.

Chapter 23

"Oh my God, Maine, a white boy likes you?" Cissy asked, in such a loud voice I'm sure Ma Bell herself stood back from the line.

"No, he doesn't. We just talked."

"That's how it starts," she warned me.

Just then, Ma came and tugged at the cord. "Maine, you've been on the phone long enough."

"I've got to go, Cissy but call me again. Tomorrow, if you can," I asked her as I reluctantly hung up. It was a shame to end it there when things were getting juicy. I had told her about me being saved and all.

"Go put on a dress. Your gammy is coming over," Ma told me.

I frowned. I could have the fairy godmother from Cinderella devise the most beautiful ball gown in the world—it wouldn't help. To put it mildly, Gammy was hard to please. And, to put it bluntly, I knew she'd get around to saying the darndest things regardless.

Still, I ran off to my room and changed from a faded T-shirt and my cut offs to a neat, a-line frock.

"Do you take drugs?" was the first question Gammy asked me.

I frowned, as I guess somehow, she'd heard about how I dove into the water without being able to swim.

Like always, she was certainly dressed in great embellishments. She had on a skirt with pleats and a sleeveless light blue blouse and pointy shoes with heels.

"Maine, to date no one has ever died of embarrassment," Gammy told me.

I nodded.

"People have died of stupidity," Gammy added. "But not embarrassment."

The breadbasket was passed around the table and I thought that since we were all seated and having deep fried trout everyone would forget about my incident. But the greasy cornmeal didn't come to the rescue, and I was stuck fielding more inspection.

"Everybody in this world ain't meant to swim," Gammy said, pointing to me with a fork. "But, if you want to swim, Charmaine, all you had to do was ask. Your own daddy was in the Navy, after all."

"She could ask me, too, Gammy," Tracy John said. "I know how."

"I do not want to learn how to swim," I said quietly.

"Well, I blame segregation. You know the school system was desegregated before the swimming pools. Ain't that a blip?"

Tracy John nearly fell out of his chair. "That's one sure blip."

"Swimming's tied up with all sorts of things. We

also weren't allowed to go bowling alleys, roller skating rinks, dance halls, of course, but we don't even do the same sort of dances. They don't want us on their rollercoaster rides. They even separated us from that - that - what's that amusement park? The one that Martin Luther King spoke about."

"I know what you mean, Ma." Uncle O said.

"Funtown. He wrote about it in 'The Letter from a Birmingham Jail'. He said how he wanted his daughter Yolanda to go to Funtown but he couldn't because it was closed to colored children."

Gammy nodded. "They wanted to keep us away from everything fun. That must be why whites are five thousand times more likely to know how to swim than us. It's a sin and a shame." She pointed to Daddy, "You couldn't swim when you joined the Navy, Payton."

"You joined the Navy without knowing how to swim?" Tracy John asked. "Unc, you are boss."

"But that's what I did sort of --" I was left mumbling.

"It was sheer force of will. There were a handful of us, like four out of the whole boot camp. They separated from everyone else and gave us some extra instruction. We did a whole lot of thrashing and fighting the water. Had to drink a lot, but we all got there with the rest of the class. Even if the swimming pools were segregated, ponds and lakes and rivers weren't segregated. My shipmates learned that way. Maine, I'll see if I can get a day off and we'll go down to the shore. Maybe I could teach you there."

Oh, no, I thought as my soul sank deeper. My father actually suggested a whole day at the hot, sandy beach – this was getting worse.

How could he look right at me and not tell him? How did he not know?

It wasn't my objective to get a tan.

Chapter 24

In Recognition of
OUTSTANDING SERVICE

We Hereby Honor
Leif Lundberg

Leif Lundberg exhibited outstanding service in assisting a young woman who was in distress. In recognition of his outstanding efforts on July 18th, 1976, in which he used his experience, training and communication skills to prevent a potential tragedy.

Thank you, Leif Lundberg, for your outstanding will to perform your duties.

I read the certificate at least a dozen times, realizing that I was the "young woman who was in distress" and that no one will ever know it. In life, we all have to *be* something but, for once, there was an inkling of joy in being in anonymity.

Finally, content after a dozen more readings of this, I bumped smack dab into Leif and his gigantic lifesaver on a rope and his whistle.

I straightened up my stance. "I'm glad you got recognition," I told him.

He smiled as he shrugged.

"Did they have a ceremony?" I asked.

He still seemed unphased. "They mentioned it during our weekly meetings."

"Your weekly lifeguard meeting?"

"Yeah, it was embarrassing."

Try being the one sinking, I thought but didn't verbalize.

"I didn't know what to say in front of everyone."

My jaw dropped at his casualness.

"You didn't have a speech written out?" I asked.

This was the second time I'd spoken to him and the second time he'd given me a double take, causing me to wonder if maybe my need for recognition was wildly out of step.

"-- Just in case, it ever should arise. Besides, you said you we're looking forward to it."

"Well, not like that. I didn't mean it like I'd said it. I don't want people to drown."

"Well, me, as a person, I didn't want to drown. Contrary to what some would believe. There's something about the water. It doesn't look threatening at all. And I'm so tall, I thought I could stand right up."

"You were on the nine feet end. How did you ever

think you could you stand up?" he asked, then his tone switched. "I'm sorry, I don't know your name?"

"Charmaine."

"That's my girlfriend's name. She goes by Lori though."

"Really? How do you get that from Charmaine?"

"What?" he asked.

"I'm Charmaine. How do you get Lori from Charmaine?"

"Oh, then I heard you wrong. It's a little hard to hear in here," he said.

The indoor pool was in a big, empty room, so the walls, ceiling and the water surface were perfect reverberation chamber.

He nodded. "You can definitely hear an echo."

We are all trapped inside a shell called race.

"Echo," I said to hear my echo of the pool's glossy surface.

"Echo," he did the same.

The sound bounced and flipped.

I asked him point blank. "So, you have a girlfriend?"

-

"He probably listens to America's top 40 with Casey Kasem," Millicent told me over the telephone that night.

"What's that?" Cissy asked Millicent. She was over my house, and we were sharing the phone's receiver.

"That's where they rundown the big rock and roll

songs."

Cissy nodded. "This is never going to work. He's rock and you're soul."

"Maine, you're all Harold Melvin and the Blue Notes and Rufus featuring Chaka Khan. He's all Seals and Croft and Peter Frampton."

Does Don Cornilus's Soul Train only come into black homes? I thought.

"It would be more far apart if he was country, and I was jazz." Johnny Cash and Miles Davis are oceans apart.

"They don't even watch the same TV shows as us."

Silently, I disagreed with my best friend as I thought of that sitcom that was such a hit at my junior high where they made it seem like living in the projects was a laugh a minute. They even called it: Good Times. Ironic much? Good times? I was never a fan of that struggle comedy complete with a police siren in the near distance, the rumble of the el train. It took place in a 600 square foot flat for the five characters. Joking about all the roaches – the sleeping quarters weren't Dynamite!

"They don't eat the same things we do," Cissy said.

"What?" I asked.

"Yeah, they love salad," Cissy clarified.

"I like salad," I said.

"Not macaroni, Maine."

"Oh, then no." Then I thought deeper. "What difference does salad make? This is the United States of

America, guys. They are all going to be our classmates in a month now, so we better learn to bend."

"Bend? That's all we've been doing since they dragged us here," Millicent said.

"Yeah." Cissy agreed.

"We never made laws not to go to school with them. We did the opposite. We wanted to go to school with them and we took all the way up to the supreme court."

"That was 50 years ago, we're all in this together. So, we might as well make the best of it."

"And they pronounce things wrong," Cissy said.

Now, this I got to hear.

"They don't even have aunts. They have ants. White people always pronounce it that way."

"Ants weren't relatives, like they were little insects who army up and invade picnics," Millicent said.

"You two need to quit," I finally said.

I hated to disagree with my two best friends when I saw them so infrequently, but it was as if listening to a record that was so broken the vinyl had all but crumbled like bacon bits then somehow stitched together and the same snatches of lyrics and kept repeating and repeating "black this" and "white that" and race race race race.

I get it. We were a homogenous lot—Baptist, pro Democratic, not prone to sunburn…but I could get along with people who didn't agree with me.

He'd said his girlfriend's name was Lorraine.

For instance, I tried to picture Lorraine. Did she have sparkling green wide eyes? A toothy smile? Did she have long flaxen flowing hair? Did she flaunt it? Did she turn on (Farrah) Fawcett? I'd always preferred a pixie haircut compared with the Rapunzel long length. Maybe, this Lori had the Dorothy Hammel bowl cut that spun about in the wind.

I thought of heading to William Penn Way High School and the herd of students pouring into the cafeteria. The white kids would have their own jocks and nerds. They didn't need us, but we needed them because they have air conditioners and full encyclopedia sets with not a single letter missing.

"What kind of a name is Leif?" Cissy asked.

"The same kind of name Cissy is," I said.

"Maine is right, he didn't pick his name. Let's be honest," Millicent said. "My grandma told me that white people always pretend to be nice."

Millicent's grandma was in her 70s, so she was born back when (I guess we were called Negroes, in 1910).

I didn't know what history books she was referring to. "No, they don't."

"No, I mean to our faces. Behind our backs, they're sneaky and I don't trust them," Millicent said.

"I still didn't see how 'no colored allowed' signs were right in your face."

"They don't want us there." Cissy rolled her eyes.

"We haven't even got there," I said.

"I'm warning you. Expect problems because they really don't want us there," Millicent said.

"Yeah, big problems," Cissy agreed.

"Well, what do you have to say?"

"I listened," I told them. But how did it equate? A white person just saved my life. How did I reconcile that?

-

That night I wrote a second entry in my diary:

I had a quick thought about something I thought I'd never think about. I'm hereby open to dating white guys.

P.S. I don't think much will ever become of this because, so far I've only met one.

Chapter 25

The veins of the clouds smeared the sky. Tracy John asked to go the long way home down by the athletic track and past the work-in-progress library to catch the demise of Dardon Junior High. The word was out that the destruction was due to start.

The area was gated off and a warning sign telling us not to enter was placed. It had started. This emblem. This legacy had begun its reduction. It was on the move toward ruins like some bombed-out post-war casualty.

Principal Abderholden was right, this was so disrespectful. It was such an insult. Our historical and cultural significance would soon be flushed down the proverbial toilet in the vague name of "progress".

Oh, and let's not forget this new school was going to have air conditioning (just in time for that sweltering, hot autumn weather?) and wall to wall carpeting (which "studies show" will move test scores remarkably?) At any rate, there was no need for the sales pitch. We didn't have a choice then, and we don't have a choice now.

Principal Abderholden had good reason to break

up that grad night. I knew he wouldn't be moving on with us to William Penn Way High School. Like a lot of black teachers and administrators after desegregation, Principal Abderholden would have a harder time finding an opening in the shake up. Mr. Mand, despite his Socialist leanings, was fantastic as our English teacher. He introduced us to Robert Frost, Maya Angelou, and Wallace Stevens. Miss Baineau, our French teacher, Mr. Gowdy, our civics teacher, and Mr. Mirabelle, our chemistry teacher... All of them would be spread to the wind. They wouldn't be joining us in the move. Nor would the administrators be kept. The new school had theirs and couldn't fit any of ours.

The promise was that this new school would take things up a level with the choices: not art but studio art, and not French and Spanish, but French, Spanish, German, and Italian.

I couldn't wait.

This merger of schools was so forced it was court ordered, still in 1976. Brown v. The Board of Education of Topeka hit the Supreme Court in 1954, all these years later, and we were still wrestling with it.

And, so, our cherished place of learning was to come down in a heap of rubble.

What I learned so far this summer was that it was better to have and not need, than to need and not have.

In front of me, they weren't builders, they were destroyers, and as far as I was concerned you must really not be wrapped too tight if you actually chose ripping places apart for a living. The carved limestone, the Greek figures—trashed. Funny, people travel thousands of miles to marvel at Machu Picchu and the Pyramids but here in America something gets to be twenty years old, and we can't wait to tear it down, all in the name of progress.

Around one, the construction workers started to clear away, I think this was their break. I hoped they'd take a long lunch—like a couple of years.

Tracy John had been cheering as he watched all the scraping and hammering. But it irked me to my soul.

<u>That</u> was *my* SCHOOL.

Chapter 26

The picture of Raymond I had been treasured. I had found charm in his large circular eyes endearingly capped by heavy, wild caterpillar black eyebrows. I only had a wallet sized photograph of him. There was a time that I had wished it was expanded to poster size.

But life tilted toward emptiness without a word from him and now I wished the picture was microscopic, or that it would totally disappear.

People come into your life and make themselves important to you and you're forced to try and forget them when they leave your life. It's so stupid.

Right after picture day, as soon as Raymond cut up the sheet of twenty, I was the first one (even before his mom even) to get this likeness.

Lately, I was inclined to keep his picture face down. In a way that made things worse because his handwritten inscription was a simple,

> To Maine,
> love forever,
> Raymond.

I wrote him something back equally as amorous

(and sappy) to him on the back of the ninth-grade photo, something about how he'd answered my prayers and made my dreams come true, but if I were to do it all over I'd state the following:

> *Dear Raymond,*
> *You're full of*
> *such*
> *bull*
> *- Maine*

Of course, there was no bucket of love. And, it wasn't like giving up on Raymond, my first love, would actually open up space for anything else. I was still unable to get my working papers cultivated to get that donut job, the free library was still closed to edification, the card deck of school ranking was about to be reshuffled (and I was gonna have to claw my way back to recognition again) and, most of all, if I ever dove again to the ocean, I'd sink like a stone.

Chapter 27

Ma was a whirlwind of activity. It was hard to catch her completely still, so I settled on finding her folding towels.

"How do you feel about white people, Ma?" I asked her.

She looked at me with knitted eyebrows and continued gathering clothing.

"I'm conducting a poll for the Philadelphia Bulletin. Your answers will remain anonymous if you like," I told her.

She handed me a pile of wash from the line. "Charmaine, you talk a lot of hogwash sometimes."

I took on the task, but I pressed on. "You grew up in the South—ever see a cross burning?"

That made her frown deepen.

"Mama, how come you never open up and let it flow?"

She shook her head, handed me a heap of wash, and told me, "There is more to life, Charmaine, than letting things flow."

-

Many more days had passed and the "Help Wanted" sign was gone from Donut World's window, taking my one dollar and 25 cents an hour dreams with it.

My eleven month younger brother, Leo, was back for the weekend. I noticed the difference in him immediately. My brother was a dancer, a mover. In my vision of him, he was always tapping, even in his sneakers.

But when I saw him that afternoon in the kitchen, he was nearly still—like a stone. Like a starfish, he was drained of expression. Was this the end result of six weeks of dance camp?

"What's the long face for?" Daddy asked Leo.

At that Leo jumped to some animation—a sudden spark of dourness. "Nash Jules Fullan," he said.

"Who's that?" I asked.

Next, came an intermission. Leo didn't answer at first. I rolled my eyes. *What's with all the pauses, Leo? Spit it out.*

"Nash Jules Fullan got the lead part I wanted," Leo said (finally). With that admitted, the floodgates were open. "The whole darn thing was a set up."

"What whole darn thing?" Daddy asked.

"It wasn't fair. Nash came to the dance camp every year, so he knows everyone. He has the in and it's unfair. They were already warmed to his style."

That made me cock my head to the side. "Is there a law that states you can't come back every year?"

"They said he got the lead last year too," Leo said.

"He must be pretty good then," Tracy John said.

I could tell that Leo didn't want to but he shrugged, exposing the fact that for once he didn't have a suitable comeback.

I shot Tracy John a look wondering if he really knew the flames he was fanning.

Daddy shook his head. "Well, one things for sure, the best you can do is your best, Leo. Now, how can you do better than that?"

Still, Leo dimmed. Still, fixed and sealed.

-

Later that evening, I had a private conversation with Leo and in it I matched his heartache as I poured out my own. I told him all of it, lingering heavy on that chance, Donut World.

"You're not old enough to work at a job, Maine. Don't you have to be 16, at least?"

I frowned. "Not if Daddy would only sign the special papers."

"He didn't want to? Why didn't he?"

"I don't know. Because donuts are dangerous."

"What?"

"Don't you know, Leo, donuts will shake off their powder and eat me instead."

That kicked Leo into some agitation. For a second, he looked at me with horror then all at once relaxed with a smirk. "Maine, I've missed you."

"And I miss Raymond."

"He's only away for the summer...You'll live."

"No, I really don't think I will."

"Maine, stay away from the deep end, and you'll be fine."

"Ma told you about that."

"Yes, and I burst out laughing. Maine, you don't want to rush to start working, you'll be working all your life," he qualified. "And don't worry about him. Raymond's true blue."

"Leo, you're not listening. I'm being conned."

"Conned?"

"Yes, conned and hoodwinked."

Leo shook his head. "It's just as well. Summer is short enough. It all goes by so fast."

"Or, not fast enough..."

Chapter 28

As if Tracy John, as opposed to me, hadn't had enough wall-to-wall activity—Ma enrolled him in youth Bible camp. I wasn't as jealous as you might think because his day was pretty much planned. Summer by this point was a few weeks shy of being done with. I'd made peace with my restlessness. My whole agitated ennui was even getting old for me.

As soon as Rev. Clee saw me he brightened, and first I thought maybe he was happy to see me outside of Sunday, he went and asked me to help with the end of summer trip.

I nodded. That's what I get for walking around looking responsible.

I put on a strained smile. "Where are we going?"

"Pete's Farm."

"Pete?" I asked. There was no need to hold out for Old McDonald's. I told him I'd be happy to do it, knowing I'd be rewarded for it, if not in this life then in the next (or, the one in the Hindu faith, they had it right).

"Charmaine, I wish I would have known that sooner, we could have used your help with the little ones."

Babysitting. I bet Daddy would have no problem if I wanted to do this all summer.

Surely, they dove deep into the scriptures with solid study but each time I swung by it seemed like they were doing something silly.

That day they were fishing ice cubes out of the basin with their bare feet—so you can imagine there were socks and sandals and sneakers everywhere. At the end of the session, there were messes everywhere, and that was AFTER the kids went around the area cleaning. Of course, that was kid clean, not really clean. There were Lincoln logs and dolls all over the floor.

Miss Greene looked about my age but was actually 19 years old and was a sophomore in college. She was big eyed and spoke very softly and baby-like. Tracy John and the other kids loved her because she was a pushover. She rolled with whatever happened. An attitude I was adverse to. Plus, she had that kind of psychosis that every woman gets at a certain age that made her think everything a child did was "adorable".

Still, I felt the need to pitch in, especially at the end when the kids dispersed and there was still much to straighten up. I held the dustpan while Miss Greene swept. Then I carried the trash bag outside and nearly fell into the rain bucket.

Miss Greene said, "That was our project for the kids. I'm sorry."

I sensed a theme. All this summer the same motif.

As I eavesdropped, I sat toward the back only half listening. The Bible stories were all so repetitive: someone's always blind or gets struck blind but then a miracle happens, and they can see. For a bunch of people roaming the desert, it amazed me how many stories involved water. There was everyone's favorite, Noah's Ark (kids especially love that one because it involved animals and rainbows). Then there's Jonah and the whale. Moses and the Red Sea. All the baptisms and foot washings.

I'm an Old Testament. I like the stories that Moses is in. Soooooooooo much excitement with the plagues and the Pharaoh.

That night I wrote a third entry in my diary:

You'll never believe this, Diary,—I fell in, again.

P. S. And, I was saved again (well, obviously).

Chapter 29

Oh, what the heck. After the summer I had, what harm would it be to collect the eggs, water the sheep and feed the pig. The bus ride to the historical farm was supposed to take one hour and ten minutes. But, I always thought the easy buses tack on another fifteen minutes to that because buses always take longer.

And, after all this, I would go back to my default "career" babysitting. I was 5'11" curving my spine into the shape of a C to relate to their shrimpy level. Five straight afternoons of bible instruction and this is the pay off? That left twenty kids about Tracy John's age. Miss Greene, Mrs. Langley, and me.

The kids filled in, they were wired, acting sprung to be leaving Dardon.

With each hill, they bounced up and down with shrieks and howls.

Let Mrs. Langley have the "Sit your bottom in the seat" duty.

Miss Greene (the pushover) just smiled.

I turned out because we were out of the city riding over the gentle hills and woods on all sides of us. Onward, to the chickens, the goats and the pigs.

The temperature was in the high nineties and the bus rattles up something called Copper Creek Road.

I had a good night's sleep, but I was always in favor of a good daydream, so all the scenery was nice and relaxing. I dreamed as the green colors passed and a cloudiness filled my brain.

"Maine, Maine, something's wrong with the driver!"

I heard a shout then Tracy John shoved me.

I jumped to my feet and ran to the front of the bus.

The bus driver was not someone I would have noticed, a friendly bear looking kind of guy. He appeared to be in good, if not excellent health, but as I approached him, it was obvious the bus driver had collapsed. On the steering wheel!

The bus sent us tossing about.

"Maine, stop this bus," Tracy John yelled, pulling at me.

"I'm trying!"

We pitched about the bus.

It was all adrenaline. My 110 pounds pushed his 250 pounds. I pushed the driver to the side, and he fell to the floor.

Panic. Sheer and utter.

Next, I rode the brakes, skid, and let travel before regaining my grip. The bus kept hitting the curb. I was afraid the bus would tumble over on its sides.

The gas pedal went faster and the steering wheel kept each slight change drastically shifting the direction.

"Try harder, Maine," Tracy John told me.

"I know. I know." And, I did try my best to master this skill that up until that day had never attempted.

"Stop the bus!"

It was then that it dawned on me there was no brake pedal; the brake was on the steering wheel.

We pitched forward then back.

To the side of me, I saw Mrs. Langley and Miss Greene tending to the driver. They were bending him forward in the middle aisles pounding on his back.

I was able to gain control, finally, and stop the bus.

I looked back and asked, "Everybody's all right?"

I scanned their distressed faces then I eyed the driver. "Is he?"

They were all too stunned to answer.

"I think he's having some sort of diabetic episode," Miss Greene said.

"D-does anyone know how to drive?" I asked.

A couple of the kids were shaking their heads. My eyes darted toward the adults. Sadly, everyone else was female. Some mothers drove but not all, not even most.

My mom never learned how to drive a regular automobile, so commanding a large vehicle was totally out of the question.

Worse had gotten worser.

I guess, we never would get to the chickens, pigs and the goats.

"I'll go and get help," I promised.

Unsteady with my footing as I disembarked the bus, I felt a hand on my shoulder.

"I'm coming with you," Tracy John volunteered.

We were out in the middle of nowhere. I didn't know if I should go up or down the road either. Tracy John cracked his head north and south. I took his hand, and I picked a direction and went with it.

-

"It'll be nightfall soon," Tracy John said, whipping his head back and forth, hypersensitive.

"What movie did you hear that in?" I asked.

"Why?"

"In the first place, Tracy John, it's noon. Night won't fall for another nine hours."

"I hope we find some help by then," Tracy John said.

I nodded, wishing I'd left him in the bus.

"Are we in Canada?"

If this was the busy Philadelphia streets they would have had people pouring out. But it wasn't and wherever we were at, it was deserted. I needed a straw hat since I was sweating. The sun had nothing to do with it. This time I didn't answer his question. I didn't know.

More paces, more yards, how many country miles?

I thought of walking him back to the bus and having him wait with everyone else. They were Tracy John's age or younger, mere tadpoles. They couldn't help me. I could get farther without him.

The bus driver, our poor bus driver sucking on orange slices down to the peel, was sweating and babbling when I'd left him. How long could he last on raisin boxes and oatmeal bars? I wondered what would be less traumatic. Supplies run low. The need for medical attention. He could have a seizure and slink into a coma. But what way to go? This narrow dirt road looked no more promising than the other slip into the dirt road.

I carried around three dimes at all times because of this exact case: an emergency. Now, if only I could get to a pay phone. I wondered if they would ever invent a telephone that you walk around with, something small and portable. That would be perfect for times like this because it's not like you need to walk around with a phone for ordinary reasons.

Just then, the back strap of my scandal broke.

Tracy John and I were stuck in the deep and immense as any woods can be, the Pennsylvania countryside with all its green. Now, I had to favor one leg as I strode.

Damn.

Chapter 30

"Maine, let's just face it: we're gonna die," Tracy John said as we continued to pace due south.

"Be optimistic, Tracy John."

"I hope we don't step on a bear trap."

"I thought you were the outdoorsy type. You always go fishing with Unc."

"That's different."

"Why?"

"Cuz I was with Unc."

"If the shoe was on the other foot, I wouldn't doubt you."

"Maine, your shoe is broken, and you don't even know where we are," Tracy John said. "Hey, maybe there was a map on the bus."

Excellent idea, that, of course, would have been of great value if he had said it 2,900 steps ago. I sighed. He was smart but a fabulous 20 minutes too late with that suggestion.

Pigs? Goats? chickens? Where are you?

The squirrels, on the side of the road, sniffed, froze then scurried away. The day was a bright smell of pine, elderberry, and learn.

The brushes thinned and I saw a brook and thankfully I saw a traditional 1800s homestead. People dressed in historic clothing, spinning and weaving in the cabin, hearth cooking and food preservation in the farmhouse and animal husbandry in the barn while Tracy John took off running.

A wagon ride through the covered bridge to see the heritage apple orchard and pond and a tour of the traditional kitchen garden or a visit to the one room school. The demonstrators at work demonstrated such as basket making, bobbin lacing, tatting, weaving, quilling, rope making and pottery.

We found it—the set of <u>Little House on the Prairie</u>.

I signed from relief as I said, "Oh, thank God."

Chapter 31

The announcer was a model of perfection with his fresh-looking haircut, close shave, shiny pressed shirt, blue silk tie, clean clipped nails, and shined shoes.

He reported: A youth vacation bible trip to a nearby farm had a brush with danger when a bus driver had a diabetic attack causing him to lose control of the wheel...

I rolled my shoulders back and patted Tracy John's afro.

We were at the sight of the "harrowing experience." Tracy John who spoke with flow was a natural. "I looked around and she grabbed the wheel, and she was driving."

"I understand that you've never driven before?"

"No I – " I started to say.

"No, she doesn't drive," Solly spoke over me. "Just Unc does."

"Unc?"

Tracy John leaned into the mic. "That's her Daddy."

The announcer nodded. "I see. Now, how can this be explained? You must have had only a split second to react. What came over you?"

"She was incredible," Tracy John said. "She saved all of us."

"Well, I –" I began.

"If she didn't take charge, we would have all gone into the river."

"There was no river, Tracy John," I corrected him.

"We would have gone over the cliff?" Tracy John asked, as if he wasn't a witness in this yarn he was spinning.

I nudged him. "Tracy John, there was no cliff."

"It was a dangerous situation. Do you look up to your cousin, Charmaine?" the announcer asked, seeming to shift in his story.

I was so determined not to be upstaged again it wasn't till I seized the microphone that I realized that this question wasn't for me.

I passed the mic Tracy John's way.

His face broke into a free smile. "Yeah, because she's eight feet tall."

Daddy nodded proudly. "Hey, now, that was all right." He turned to Ma. "Can you believe it, Miss Sweet Thang?"

Ma, having said about a half dozen, "Oh, my Lords" and two "My Mys" during the airing, now, didn't answer. She was too busy dabbing her eyes. Would she ever get to the point where she could hold the waterworks?

"It's so beautiful," Ma finally got out. "So beautiful."

"Does Horace get to see us on TV?" Tracy John

asked.

I didn't have the heart to tell him they didn't get channel 10 way in Hawaii.

Once again, I felt sighted, all but erased. If only Tracy John wasn't so lovable looking, I'm sure my more offbeat presence would have gotten more face time.

Tracy John's cheeks looked even plumper on screen and those eyes of his looked so warm and bright. W.C. Fields was right, "Never work with children or animals."

Still, it was something, to be on TV and all. Broadcast all over the Delaware Valley. Sandwiched after the run down and before getting back to how Jimmy Carter was polling against Gerald Ford (I was rooting for the peanut farmer because I didn't approve of Ford or how he fell into the office of president without getting a single vote – Thank you, Nixon.) was an update from sportscasters Quebec on how well our country was doing in the Olympics.

The camera captured us so I was assured we would also be in the newspaper in the coming days and in fact we were. We made the front page (of the B section).

Soon the phone rang off nonstop. I got calls from Gammy, Millicent, Cissy, Principal Aberholden, and someone I really didn't expect, Raymond's mother, called me.

Stay gracious, Charmaine. Don't go off on this lady

about how her son filled my head with all these fantasies about how much he cared, how devoted he was and then all summer he ditched me.

She told me the exact date Raymond would be back in town.

August 26th. Five days before the start of school.

"Oh, boy, Mrs. Newell, I can't wait to see your son," I said through gritted teeth.

Chapter 32

"If Jesus was on the boat with them, what did they have to worry about?" Rev. Clee asked.

The rest of the time was taken up by scripture reference: Luke 8:22 to 8:25 – the story of the storm.

"Have no fear Jesus was on the boat with his apostles." Rev. Clee continued, "Jesus is always on the boat with us. He is on the boat of life with us. But still we worry. We worry about it. We worry about drowning, but Jesus is right by your side."

"He is?" a stray person asked.

Rev. Clee doubled down. "He is!"

There was a round of "Amens" from the congregation and the reverend asked me to please stand.

I was reluctant. If I would have known this was going to happen, I would have worn that blue dress instead of this mauve one – blue was my color.

"Charmaine, please stand up here to be recognized." Well, since he insisted, I rose to get my due.

I got so many hugs and thank yous and pats on the back UNTIL the bus driver arrived at this stop – things as they were, he was just out of the hospital. So much for my plans, which were the same plans so long ago. He was completely healed.

How different he looked out of his uniform and in an orange three-piece suit with wide lapel and flared pants. It was weird to see him standing upright and his eyes wide open.

A rush of excitement shot through the congregation. And, in that second, I lost my entire fan base.

They flocked to him like he was Lazarus of Bethany.

And there I was as forsaken as Job.

Upstaged, again...

-

Later that night my hand held the pen, but I couldn't find the energy to glide it across the diary's page. There were precious few days left of the summer and there were only three entries made. Why was I so literally constipated, verbally? Or should I say literally constipated, literally.

Tracy John came bursting into the room as if on a mission.

"I know what you can be, Maine."

I grabbed him back. "For Halloween"

He shook me off and grabbed me again. "No, for life."

"Okay, Tracy John. What should I be when I grow up?"

"A preacher."

Before I rushed in to say that wasn't a job, it was a calling and it wasn't like someone could say *hey, I think you'd make a great Blank – you have to wait for a sign, a divine sign.*

"Well, what do you think?" Tracy John asked.

I took out my palms and struck a beatific expression. "And the angels sing."

Chapter 33

Behind our glasses, our eyes meet. He came toward me dressed in a Hawaii shirt and dungarees.

"Charmaine, it's so wonderful to see you after such a long time."

My heart hammered its beat, but not in a good way. My throat was clogged. I wasn't about to pretend that I didn't have a problem with him. I was fuming. "Raymond, you are the biggest jerk in the world."

The wide beam left his face. "What?"

"You heard me!"

"But I don't understand. What did I do?"

"What did you do? That's the point—you didn't."

His glasses slipped down his nose a bit. "Charmaine, I didn't what?"

"You forgot all about me."

"I did?"

"Yes, you did. And you know it."

Raymond adjusted his glasses. "No, I don't know, Charmaine."

"Yes, you do!"

"No, I don't know what I did to you."

"You don't?"

"Yes," he said, then shook his head furiously. "I mean, no. Maine–"

"How could you not even send me a letter when you knew letters were the one way, the only way you could communicate with me."

A lot of horror swept over his whole being.

"Good confused face, faker." I went to the window and wiped the frame which was clouded from moisture. Then I wiped a stray tear from my eye.

"Maine, it was your letters that stopped coming."

I looked back over my shoulder. "Because your letters never came."

He came toward me and touched the middle of my back. "But I—I wrote to you each and every evening. I poured myself into each letter."

I kept my back to him. "Well, I never got a one."

He spun me around, he touched his hand to my chin to lift it... "Maine, there must be some explanation."

My eyebrows rose then narrowed.

I didn't know what to believe. The entire summer had passed, and I'd used that time to distance myself from Raymond, to divorce him from my memory and now he had the nerve to sweep in with not even a concrete explanation. I couldn't give in. I had to remain strong. I had to hold the line so I said, "Like what, Raymond, what? What is your explanation?"

He stepped back a little and placed his hands at his sides.

"I don't know, Maine, but this I swear --" Raymond

said and right then his voice broke a bit. "As Helena said in <u>A Midsummer Night's Dream</u> 'I'll follow thee and make a heaven of hell,/ To die upon the hand I love so well'."

For a moment, I felt like I was up in a hot air balloon. Floating, with blazing fire underneath me.

"Oh, Raymond," I said as I sort of melted.

I surrendered to his embrace, rested my cheeks against his, at peace with my choice.

Chapter 34

Always wear nice clothes on the first day of school because you want to make a good impression—no dungarees, no funny T-shirts. I opted for an earth toned, butterfly collared blouse and long, flowing skirt.

I did the new thing of waiting at the school bus stop and I looked up at the sky. The glow and bright of summer had had the monotony of hard and gray winter. I was glad this limbo was over. I smelled chrysanthemums marigolds— some stubborn autumnal fragrance—in the morning air, strong as steam.

This new school was going to be great because it was next and therefore, I had no alternative but to make it great.

In life, we all have a bus to board. In fact, we have many.

Millicent and Cissy came along.

Soon, we were jumping up and down in a tight lock.

"Oh, my God, Maine, when did you turn into Cicely Tyson?" Millicent asked.

"You do look great, Maine," Cissy said.

"Me? You two, too. We are goddesses!" I proclaimed.

Millicent had on a pastel knee length shift dress

with cap sleeves.

Cissy had peasant blouses with a swinging skirt.

"You guys look fantastic too. I missed you so much!"

We hugged again.

Sure, I never learned to swim, and I washed my anger with Raymond, never made donuts and never got my $1.25 an hour. My valedictorian reign was over, and a new struggle would begin.

If I learned anything from this summer, it was to face the unknown. Stand up straight, throw your shoulders back, then dive in, headfirst – and make a splash.

THE END

About the Author

Allison Whittenberg won the John Steinbeck Writing Award, Judith Siegel Pearson Award, and several Pushcart Prize nominations. Her novels include *Sweet Thang, Hollywood and Maine, Life is Fine, Tutored* through Random House. Her collection of short stories *Carnival of Reality* and her novella *Sane Ayslum* were published by Apprentice House Press. She currently teaches creative writing in Drexel University's MFA program.

Apprentice
House Press
Loyola University Maryland

Apprentice House is the country's only campus-based, student-staffed book publishing company. Directed by professors and industry professionals, it is a nonprofit activity of the Communication Department at Loyola University Maryland.

Using state-of-the-art technology and an experiential learning model of education, Apprentice House publishes books in untraditional ways. This dual responsibility as publishers and educators creates an unprecedented collaborative environment among faculty and students, while teaching tomorrow's editors, designers, and marketers.

Eclectic and provocative, Apprentice House titles intend to entertain as well as spark dialogue on a variety of topics. Financial contributions to sustain the press's work are welcomed. Contributions are tax deductible to the fullest extent allowed by the IRS.

To learn more about Apprentice House books or to obtain submission guidelines, please visit www.apprenticehouse.com.